There are petrol barrels across the road. Our car stops. Three men in shabby grey uniforms open the doors and wave guns in our faces. They reach in and pull us out by our shoulders. We never see our driver's face or the guide's to know whether this ambush has been expected or is a terror for them too. Towels are put over our heads, our wrists bound, and we're pulled past the petrol barrels up onto the back of a lorry. There's shouting – harsh orders from them, terrified shouts from us. What did I manage? 'Keep calm, do as they say.' Something like that. There's the hollow sound of the petrol barrels being tipped over and rolled to the roadside and then the lorry fires into life. I see worn black boots and metal gun barrels resting on knees. My own tied hands are shaking. I glimpse other hands reaching for our bags and rifling through them; catch that twist of a lower body as something is thrown far away.

Also available by Tom Pow and published by Random House Children's Books:

SCABBIT ISLE

'Exquisitely written . . . a short classic' *Literary Review*

'Compelling and beautifully written' Michael Morpurgo, *Children's Laureate (2003–2005)*

'So well-written it makes most books look clumsy and heavy-footed in comparison' *Achuka*

'The main characters are well-drawn in this intelligently constructed debut novel' *Books for Keeps*

'A powerful ghost story . . . enjoyable and engagingly streetwise' *Irish Times*

THE PACK

'Disturbing and thought-provoking, and the story-telling powerful' *The Bookseller*

'*The Pack* is one of the best books of its kind' *The Scotsman*

'The author's insight into the mind of wild dogs is one of the novel's best features. Like Mad Max for kids, this is savagely exciting, its violence and tension underscored by spare, evocative writing and a deep moral sense' Amanda Craig, *The Times*

'An intelligent, provocative and compulsive read' *School Librarian*

'[Tom Pow] has powerful philosophical points to make about the nature of story and identity, and of loyalty and trust, but never at the expense of what is a demanding and compelling plot. His language remains that of the poet – self-conscious in the best sense of the term, constantly nurturing both characters and ideas. Heartfelt and beautifully descriptive, it offers a narrative path which will encourage young readers into accepting the undoubted challenges of this passionate, often troubling novel' Lindsey Fraser, *Scottish Review of Books*

CAPTIVES

TOM POW

CORGI BOOKS

CAPTIVES
A Corgi Book 978 0 552 55547 0 (from January 2007)
0 552 55547 9

Published in Great Britain by Corgi Books,
an imprint of Random House Children's Books

This edition published 2006

1 3 5 7 9 10 8 6 4 2

Papers used by Random House Children's Books are natural, recyclable products made from wood grown in sustainable forests. The manufacuring processes conform to the environmental regulations of the country of origin.

Set in 11/15pt Baskerville Classico by
Falcon Oast Graphic Art Ltd.

Corgi Books are published by Random House Children's Books,
61–63 Uxbridge Road, London W5 5SA,
a division of The Random House Group Ltd,
in Australia by Random House Australia (Pty) Ltd,
20 Alfred Street, Milsons Point, Sydney, NSW 2061, Australia,
in New Zealand by Random House New Zealand Ltd,
18 Poland Road, Glenfield, Auckland 10, New Zealand,
in South Africa by Random House (Pty) Ltd,
Isle of Houghton, Corner Boundary Road & Carse O'Gowrie,
Houghton 2198, South Africa
and in India by Random House India Pvt Ltd,
301 World Trade Tower, Hotel Intercontinental Grand Complex,
Barakhamba Lane, New Delhi 110001, India

THE RANDOM HOUSE GROUP Limited Reg. No. 954009
www.**kids**at**randomhouse**.co.uk

A CIP catalogue record for this book is available from the British Library.

Printed and bound in Great Britain by
Cox & Wyman Ltd, Reading, Berkshire.

Captives *is for Delia Huddy*
and for my family, Julie, Cameron and Jenny

ACKNOWLEDGEMENTS

I'd like to thank all those responsible for the expert advice I received in the writing of *Captives*. Dr Philip Clayton answered with his usual clarity a number of medical questions I had. Alastair Reid and Professor Mike Gonzalez helped me immeasurably with matters linguistic and cultural. Together with Professor W. George Lovell and Leslie Clark, Alastair and Mike have shared their deep knowledge of Latin America with me over the years. Individually and collectively they have enlarged my sense of the possible. *Compañeros*.

I began writing *Captives* while in Cuba thanks to a Scottish Arts Council Writer's Bursary. I wish to acknowledge that here and also to thank Glasgow University Crichton Campus for granting me time away from work.

I am grateful to Harriet Wilson and Delia Huddy for their enthusiasm for *Captives* in its initial stages. I wish to thank my editor, Lucy Walker, for the sensitivity of her work on the novel and my agent, Jenny Brown, for her unfailing support.

Delia Huddy showed concern for *Captives*, even when facing the hospital operation from which she never recovered. This novel is for her and, as ever, with love and gratitude, for my family – Julie, Cameron and Jenny.

Tom Pow
Dumfries, Feb 2006

CONTENTS

In the high sierras
Where juniper fills the air
Or in the deep green forest
Where the water's at its coolest – there
And around each blue fringe
Of this, our island home,
You cannot help but hear
The bones of the dead ask
As if in prayer
What have you done
With our gifts? The wind
Thickens in the south. Clear your throat –
It is time you prepared an answer.

Rafael Portuondo

PROLOGUE

His father came on, paused briefly at the top of the stairs, as he would have been told to do, and acknowledged the studio audience's applause. He did so with a cursory nod of the head – he was not a pop star after all – and then came down the stairs to join Callaghan, the host. To this part at least, Martin knew, he would have given a lot of thought, and he took the stairs lightly and quickly – a man of energy and action.

He shook hands with Callaghan, eased himself onto the black leather chair and checked the lie of his jacket. Martin leaned back on his bed and pressed the volume control of his small bracketed TV up a couple of notches.

'Well, Tony, as we said in our intro there, it is an amazing story – or perhaps *drama* would be the better description.'

'Yes, it is. It sometimes seems like a dream now.'

'Or a nightmare, more like?'

'Indeed, a nightmare. An absolute nightmare.' Martin saw his father recognize the mistake he had made and his quickness in rectifying it. They had to get the category right after all – file under *nightmare*, not dream.

'Well, Tony, just to take you back to the island of Santa Clara for a moment and to remind us all what you went through, here's the photograph of you and the other hostages that was syndicated around the world.'

A large projection showed a handful of glum westerners in shorts and T-shirts in a forest setting. Two men, one heavily bearded, and a woman stood behind a boy squatting between another woman and a girl. The girl's grimace could almost be mistaken for a smile.

'You can see in your faces the torment you were going through. And that was what – a week or so after your capture?'

'Yes, that was after a week. It's hard to look at that now, you know, to see how worn down we all look, yet there were still another three weeks to go before we were freed.'

'And living all that time not knowing whether you'd ever get out alive?'

'Exactly. A month doesn't sound like a long time – but in those circumstances it felt like . . . well . . . for ever.'

For Martin, the shock of the picture still lay mostly in seeing himself there in the jungle, squatting beside Louise. If it was a dream to him, the clearest part of it was that: their thighs touching – a small nakedness, this, but one that stood for all the strange intimacies they had shared.

As for his father, the man in the picture was closer to the one he knew – or had known – than the man on television with his elegant black suit, the polished black loafers and the clean-shaven face. The open-necked white shirt Martin recognized as another gesture to the kind of man his father was: successful, but still very much an individual.

It was a small concession, but an important one, for it gave Martin the only link between this man and the father he had known: the bearded, always dishevelled father, who was beginning to sigh into middle age, who found teaching less of a satisfaction and more of a drudge; whose war with the head over his wearing of sandals to work had become less a point of principle and more a distraction from the fact that, the sandals apart, he found less and less to engage his passions.

The screen cleared.

'As I said, Tony, that picture was in newspapers around the world, but what made your story such a drama for us all was the televised plea by your younger son, Nick.'

His father was nodding. 'Yes, of course, we knew nothing about it, but–'

'If you can bear to watch it one more time . . .'

Martin grimaced as, on the large projection screen, his thirteen-year-old brother appeared wearing a football shirt before a battery of cameras and microphones. They missed out the part where the MP had spoken of the unusualness of this 'event', while stressing that the family, and Nick in particular, wanted to do anything it could to advance the safe release of the hostages.

'I don't know,' Nick began hesitantly, his eyes on the paper before him, as the Spanish subtitles ran along the bottom of the screen – '*No sé si recibirás este mensaje, pero . . .*' – 'I don't know if you'll get this message, but if you do, please set my family, and the other family, free unharmed. You've made your point, and my family have never done anything wrong, so please, they don't deserve to suffer any more, and if they can see this at all' – and here his face lifted; a boy's face bathed in light and tears – 'love you, Mum, Dad, Martin, and I miss you so much. Come home safely . . .' His uncle Ralph's arm came around him then and Nick slumped forward, burying his face in his hands.

It was some performance, thought Martin, even seeing it for the umpteenth time. He could be sure that downstairs his mother would be wiping the tears from her eyes and cuddling Nick against her on the sofa.

Martin's father had dipped his chin into his chest, in an act of gathering himself before the next question.

'You must be very proud of your son, Tony.'

His father lifted his head. 'Yes, very. Of both of them.'

Oh, hurray, thought Martin.

'Yes, of course, the whole experience must have been a terrible one for your older son, Martin. How's he doing?'

'He's doing just fine. I think, after all that time

living so close together, he's enjoying finding his own space again.'

'Of course, no matter what happens to them, "own space" at that age is important, isn't it?'

'Seems to be, yes.'

'I mean, our son treats us like meals on wheels and the closest he gets to the wilderness is a mooch around the park with his mates.'

It was the light part of the interview: both men were smiling and the audience laughed. So what, if Martin had been skated over? He knew there were barbs to come and he worried for his father, now looking so relaxed, so like a real celebrity on Callaghan's *Saturday Night Talk Show*.

'Now, Tony, the diary. You don't take any prisoners yourself.' Callaghan smiled, liking the line.

His father frowned. 'I wouldn't put it like that. I just think that if you are going to do something like this, there's no point if you're not going to be honest.'

'Even about your wife. You *are* a brave man, Tony.'

'Yes, well . . .' said his father, pausing to choose his words. 'I happen to think my wife is a very brave woman too. She was just as determined that the truth be told as I was.'

'Agreed, Tony, agreed. But just on that point, is the

diary word for word as you wrote it? I mean, it must have been written in very trying circumstances, yet there's no end of detail in it.'

'That's true, and obviously, for publication, parts of it have had to be worked up and clarified for the reader – while remaining true to the experience.'

'I see,' said Callaghan with a twinkle in his eyes. 'Tony, the diary's been a great success, hasn't it?'

'Well, I . . .' and his father smiled faintly.

'Oh, don't be so modest. Wherever it's been serialized, newspaper and magazine sales have rocketed. And it's been translated into Lord knows how many languages.'

'Six, so far,' said his father. It was a brief flare of pride; forgivable if you knew that this was a writer who'd waited most of his adult life to be published. But it was a miscalculation Martin knew his father would pay for.

'Six, begorra! And there's talk of it being turned into a book and a film. Who do you see playing yourself? George Clooney?'

His father didn't rise to that one, thankfully, only smiled out of politeness.

'I think it just happens to be a story people can

identify with. You know, ordinary people in an extraordinary situation.'

'Nightmare, as you say, nightmare.'

Callaghan had said it twice, as far as Martin could tell, to let the word settle, to act as a brake on all that had gone before. Because now, with the smell of blood in the air, he was smiling sympathetically.

'Tony, if we may' – and he paused, as if the next words were hard to find – 'just touch on the rather public falling out between you and the Deschamps family . . .'

'Of course, but can I say now that nothing saddens me more than this, after all we went through together?'

'I'm sure we all' – Callaghan swept an arm round the audience – 'understand that. Nevertheless, what do you say to their accusations that you are profiteering from their misery? I mean, you *are* making a profit, aren't you? Six translations and counting, as you said yourself.'

There was a glow about Callaghan now, his silver hair still immaculate, his suit crisp, as Martin's father began to shift uncomfortably, out of his depth, in his ill-fitting black designer suit.

'No, I wouldn't deny that the diary has made money.'

'And the Deschamps, as you know, Tony, claim that that was your intention from the start. They say that the only "voice" speaking to you out there was one saying you could make a lot of money out of the experience – that you concentrated your efforts on your diary to the exclusion of all else.'

'That's crazy – I mean, not crazy, but absolutely mistaken. After all, none of us had any idea we were going to get out of there alive. I just thought that if we did, then it was – and is – a story that deserves to be told. As a tribute to everything we went through and especially . . .'

'To little Louise.'

'To Louise, yes.'

'Because, Lord, it must have been horrendous never knowing if Nick was alive or dead – but that's not quite the same as losing a daughter.'

Martin saw the statement as a trap; something to draw some ire from his father or a few more beads of sweat under the lights. His father swallowed and remained calm.

'I would never, in a million years, claim that it was. And I don't think anything I've written or said would give that impression.'

It was, however, the impression, or something like

it, the Deschamps had taken. Martin glanced to the foot of his bed, where the crumpled newspaper article was spread out. He'd saved it from the bin into which his mother had thrown it. AT OUR DAUGHTER'S COST, read the banner headline. Below it, the Deschamps, recently separated ("'The loss of Louise,' Melanie Deschamps tells us, 'was a pain we just couldn't share . . .'"), outlined the case against Tony Phillips and his wife, Carol. Whenever there was work to be done – the setting up of a camp, the digging of a latrine, the gathering of firewood – the Deschamps claimed, Tony Phillips would be lost in his diary and his wife in those crude line drawings which now illustrated it.

The girl who appeared in the main photograph – there was a smaller one inset of the smiling family of three – was naturally more groomed than she had looked in the famous *Captives* photograph. This was a school photograph after all. She wore her auburn hair long over her shoulders: the studio lighting had emphasized its reddish hue. Martin remembered the day when she'd insisted it be shorn because of the heat. He remembered her long neck; the trail of light hairs that led down to her back.

The uniform and the pose naturally gave the

picture a formality, but there was a light in her eyes, an openness that took in the joking photographer. To those who could see it, there was the same light in the eyes of the girl whose knee lay against his in that forest – a slight pressure he felt more keenly than almost anything that had touched him in all the days since.

There had been the briefest pause in the interview, as if Callaghan knew this was the time to let Martin's father off the leash; either to offer a credible defence or to bury himself. His father took his chance.

'Can I say here, as I've said before, that I – or any other person with an ounce of feeling – would do anything to change the end of the story? But fighting isn't going to bring Louise back. As for profits, I've offered to set up a scholarship or some kind of trust fund in Louise's name as a memorial–'

'Which her family reject.'

'Unfortunately, at the moment, yes.'

'What reasons do they give for this decision?'

'I really don't want to speak for the Deschamps. They have their reasons. All I would say is that I too recognize a young life is beyond price.'

There were a few claps from the audience, during which his father turned to the side table, lifted the tumbler and took a good gulp of water.

'I'm sure we all agree with that sentiment. Lastly, Tony, what do you say to their criticism that you present the guerrillas in a favourable light?'

Oh, Dad, you old hippy, Martin thought, you've been rumbled.

'Oh, that. Well, naturally, I utterly condemn their actions. I hope that's clear in the diary.'

'Certainly it is. But there's also a way in which their leader emerges as a figure of dignity, a poet to boot – he and his sidekick, Maria.'

'Maria couldn't really be described as—' his father began, then changed his mind. He sensed time was running out. And he had an important point to make.

'I don't know about that,' he said. 'I think that's really for the reader to decide.'

His father's instincts had been right. For immediately, Callaghan was thanking his father for 'coming on the show' and 'being so candid' and 'sharing his incredible story with us all on such an *un-tropical* night'. 'Good luck with the film' was his final comment, a clear indication of the line he had been following throughout the interview. But, as his father nodded briefly at the audience's applause and shook Callaghan's hand, Martin thought it could have been a lot worse, and his last answer about 'letting the reader decide' had been a good one.

He flicked off the TV and reached for the stack of four Sunday supplements which currently made up the published diary. But there were steps on the stairs. He threw part of his bedcover over the magazines. His mother opened the door, enough to pop her head in.

'Did you see it?' she asked.

'Uh-huh.'

'What did you think?'

'I thought he came out of it OK.'

'Me too. Quite a relief.'

They exchanged fleeting smiles.

'Aren't you going to come down to join us?'

Us.

'Nick would like that. Dad'll be home soon. We could watch a video.'

'It's a DVD these days, Mum.'

'Yes, sorry, of course, a DVD.'

'Maybe later.'

'All right . . . You OK up here? Warm enough? It's perishing outside.'

'I'm fine. Like, we do have central heating.'

'Yes, sorry, of course. What are you going to be doing?'

'Just reading. Listening to music.'

'Oh.'

His mother stood in the doorway in silence, as if frozen there.

'Mum.'

'Yes, Martin.'

'Is there anything else?'

'No. Nothing. Just wondering what you're reading.'

'Just stuff.'

'Oh well.' She had moved into the room now and reached out a hand to stroke his hair, but he bent his head away from her.

'Sure you're all right?'

'Perfectly. Now please, Mum . . .'

His mother gave him one last weak smile and closed the door after her.

The diaries were published in magazine form as *Exclusive: Captives,* a lurid red title slantwise across the photograph of them all hunkering down in the forest. Below the photograph, *The Diary by Tony Phillips* was in sober black lettering. Of course, the published diaries could not show what the original diary did in its thick black notebook: namely, a deep triple scoring under the previous day's entry, an over-poetic description of a day spent snorkelling in clear, blue waters. These scores, more eloquently than anything else, marked the fearful border they had all crossed. *Jesus, what has happened? What will happen now?*

Martin knew that finally he had to read the diaries for himself. It had been easier till now to let his father speak for them all – it had after all been a story his father was desperate to tell. But now was the time to get the measure of his father's story and to test it against the one he had pieced together for himself. He was aware of the tangled landscape he would have to enter once more and didn't know quite what he would find there – what false trails his father might have laid. He took a deep breath and opened the magazine.

Naturally enough, as his father had admitted openly, the diaries had been rewritten – 'lightly edited', the editor more guardedly claimed – for publication, and there was evidence of the dead hand of a sub-editor at work in each of the headings. But it was clear to Martin that his father had thought long and hard about the best way into the story. In the end he had discovered that the best way in was simply to highlight the dilemma of where to start and to give the story straight . . .

PART ONE
THE DIARIES

CAPTIVES 1
THE NIGHTMARE BEGINS

Day One

God, where to begin? How to write of this horror? We're kidnapped – held hostage – Carol, Martin and me. We don't know where Nick is, but pray he's escaped all this. There's a great need, in spite of everything, to keep calm. Perhaps the diary can help to order my thoughts, to keep a hold on what's happening to us.

Two days ago – only two days? – we turned up at Island Adventure to take up our booking of two days' trekking in the National Park. There was another family going – a Frenchman, his American wife and their daughter, who's sixteen or so: Martin's age. The Frenchman is fair, tall and athletic – the kind who looks as if he could walk all day – and I noted a small wave of anxiety cross Carol's face. I told her to take her measure not from him, but from his wife – already you could see sweat gathering behind her dimpled knees and edging the broad hairband that fought to contain the wild curls of her hair. Besides, I pointed out, there was also a couple in early retirement, the Lehmans, who we'd eaten with at the hotel the previous evening.

There was the usual lack of urgency. A small group of men in T-shirts and baseball caps came and went, greeting each other – *Buenos días, qué pasa?* etc. – the smiles broadening the more we looked at our watches. But I've learned that's the way here; eventually things do happen. So we sat in the shade of the dingy office of Island Adventure – I could laugh at the name now! – our overnight packs by our sides, made small talk with the other couples and waited. We learned the other family's name was Deschamps – Jacques and Melanie. After a while their daughter, Louise, sighed loudly and went outside to sit on the wooden steps.

Just when Martin and Nick had put that 'Come on, Dad, make something happen!' look on their faces, three battered old taxis drew up. The man who'd introduced himself to us as 'Gabriel, your guide' – a thin, jaundiced-looking man, who'd been passing the time scribbling notes and numbers on scraps of paper – came out of the shadows and told us the taxis would take us to the start of the trail. 'Do we really need three taxis?' I said. I mean, I've seen them pack six people and their luggage into an average-sized family car.

'*Seguro*,' the guide said. 'Is better for you, no?'

'*Que faire?*' I said to the Frenchman and was immediately embarrassed, as he speaks perfect English, though still with a trace of accent. He shrugged.

'Please,' said Carol, 'we've waited long enough. Don't start an argument over nothing.'

'Nothing, yes,' said the guide, and smiled weakly at Carol. I felt irritation rise in me, but then again, what was the point? We'd paid in dollars beforehand and I couldn't think how they could profit from us further – but I wouldn't have put it past them to try. We grabbed our bags and stepped outside the office into the morning sun. The white face of the church was dazzling.

Nick, Mr Sociable, said he'd go last with the Lehmans. They were delighted: 'Hey, we're a family too!' We got into the cars – smelling of hot earth and rubber – and soon were heading along the waterfront and out of town. We held onto the seats as the car rolled to avoid potholes, lorries packed with people, bicycles, walkers. The driver smiled at us in his mirror, his eyes masked by sunglasses. Our guide, who was sitting beside him, turned round once to apologize for the state of their roads. As we left the coast and cleared most of the signs of small villages, the road got even rougher, the vegetation denser, and I felt excitement at the promise of adventure.

What happened next is a blur.

There are petrol barrels across the road. Our car stops. I glance behind and see the Deschamps' car right behind us. It's a large saloon and I can't see past it to the Lehmans' taxi. Shadows cross the windows of our car. Three men in shabby grey uniforms open the doors and wave guns in our faces. They reach in and pull us out by our shoulders. We never see our driver's face or the guide's to know whether this ambush has been expected or is a terror for them too. Towels are put over our heads, our wrists bound, and we're pulled past the petrol barrels up onto the back of a lorry. There's shouting – harsh orders from them, terrified shouts from us. What did I manage? 'Keep calm, do as they say.' Something like that. There's the hollow sound of the petrol barrels being tipped over and rolled to the roadside and then the lorry fires into life. From beneath the rim of my hood I see Martin has a trickle of blood from a gash on his shin, I imagine from when he's been pushed into the back of the lorry. I also see worn black boots and metal gun barrels resting on knees. My own tied hands are shaking. I glimpse other hands reaching for our bags and rifling through them; catch that twist of a lower body as something is thrown far away.

We continue down the road for another few miles. This driver's not concerned with avoiding pot-holes and we roll into each other helplessly. The hoods have made us silent, each of us locked in our own terror. The only sounds that escape are either curses or prayers: 'Jesus, Jesus, what's happening?'

The lorry slows, turns and dips into a ditch with such suddenness, we're all thrown forward. It feels as if the lorry could roll over completely. 'Save us!' shouts Carol. Our guards push us back and the lorry revs till its front wheels are pushed out and it bucks and rolls its way across what I realize is a ford, and finally we're off the road and onto a dirt track. I tilt my head back and see a half moon of green and the red track lengthening behind us. After half an hour or so of this, the towels are removed from our heads. For a few seconds, sunlight blinds us.

Carol's wide-eyed, frozen with horror, even as she's jiggled about on the lorry.

'Look,' I say, 'maybe it's a good thing he's not here. He's not been taken. He must have got away. With the Lehmans.'

But it's as if she hasn't heard me.

'Nick, Nick, *Nick*.' The last word she almost screams, and one of the captors frowns at her and wags a finger.

'Oh my God,' she says. 'Oh my God.'

She's still saying that as the lorry gutters to a halt and they pull us down off it by our shoulders, and throw our packs after us. One of the men takes my wrists and, with a machete, slices through the twine that binds them. The machete's a polished blade the length of my forearm – the man half smiles as he gestures to the others to hold out their hands too. We glance at each other – six of us – through faces stained with dirt and sweat and tears. The lorry turns, the dust settles and we start up a narrow track, heading for the hills.

'Oh, God, where can Nick be? Pray that he's safe.'

There are five guerrillas – what else can they be? – three men, a woman and a youngster who could be little older than Martin. But they're all armed with light machine guns and we are all – the Deschamps and us – terrified.

The woman looks at Martin's shin as if in disgust. We wait as she takes a tube of something and a bandage out of her backpack and hands them roughly to Carol.

'Bind tight,' the boy says. 'Take no chances in this place.' He speaks each word clearly and frowns to make his point.

'Take no chances,' Carol repeats to herself. 'Take no chances. Take no chances.' She looks a slight and fragile figure, kneeling before Martin, binding his wound.

When it's done, I squeeze Carol's arm and Martin's and I note Jacques does the same to his wife and daughter. I think panic has silenced us all.

What surprises me is that we're still in the farmed fringes of the foothills. We walk through fields where cows are pastured and pass the occasional simple farm with a couple of plots fenced in by cacti and pigs rooting about outside. Sometimes there's someone working, cutting at an old tree with a machete or hoeing the red earth. They look up and wave their machetes at us. Our captors wave casually back, as if we're all just out for a stroll.

We're not. A dog runs too close to us, barking. One of the men, the huge black one, grabs the back of its neck and slits its throat with his machete. There's a gush of blood, then the carcass is thrown into the undergrowth. Carol leans into me, but we daren't stop.

We walk the rest of that day in our enforced silence – fear has given us all the energy, for the pace is as brisk as the slopes allow and we don't stop for rest. Finally we reach two old shelters in a clearing – simple struts designed to support a roof of palm leaves. They've not been used for a long time. The palms are brittle, the ash from the fire trampled into the earth. In one shelter a rusted old pot is tipped on its side. We eat what we've brought with us for lunch – a ham sandwich each – with what's left of our bottled water. One of them comes over to us with the boy. He is thirty or so, with dark brown cropped hair and the beginnings of a beard. Without raising his voice, he has issued most of the day's orders. The boy tells us we are to do as we're told and nothing will happen to us. But we must expect to be with them for quite some time.

'What do you want of us?' says Jacques. 'Let our wives and children go.'

But the leader shakes his head.

'You are to ask no questions,' says the boy. 'You,' he says to the Deschamps, 'other shelter. Sleep now.'

We spread out our cotton sleeping bags on the earth. The sun is gone, as quickly as if the leader took it with him when he turned his back on us.

'How's your leg?' I ask Martin, knowing there's a million questions I could ask, but am too scared to raise for his sake, for Carol's, for mine.

'It'll be OK.'

We sleep with Martin between us, sleep out of utter exhaustion. During the black night, I think I must have dreamed this. The dawn brings the truth that the nightmare is real.

Day Two

We walk another day along forest tracks, till our muscles ache and our clothes stick to us. We stop in a clearing – I can't tell one from another – and make a kind of encampment.

'You must build two shelters – like last night,' says the boy, and one of the men, the one who killed the dog, hands Jacques a machete, handle first, with a slight smile. Jacques glances at me, taken aback. But should either of us have been surprised? Earlier in the day we climbed up to a kind of saddle in the hills that gave us a view of the valley and beyond. Nothing. Nothing but thick forest in every direction. Through the boy, the leader told us that if we run we are lost, and we put the rest of the group in danger. Then he tapped his gun, as a warning. Still, though they keep their guns with them at all times, they point them at us a good deal less and they clearly don't fear giving us a machete. Or letting us go a little off the trail to do our business. Nor do they make any effort to prevent us hearing their names. Between us, we have worked out that the leader is called Rafael and the boy Eduardo. The woman's name is Maria and the names we had to work hardest to get are 'the silent watchers' – as we call them – Miguel, the dog-killer, and El something or other.

We all do our bit in constructing the shelter, but Jacques especially sets about the task as if to show them what we are made of. Tall and muscular, he was born, you would think, to wield a machete – he knows the proper weight to put behind it and each stroke falls with the same accuracy. He strips branches for uprights and makes niches to slot in the smaller branches, which will support the thatch of palm leaves.

'One here, here, here and here.' Two of us to each one, we grip the uprights and drive our weight down on them, turning as we do so, till they are rooted in the earth. The guerrillas have finished their shelter. They sit a little away, talking and occasionally looking across at us. Once there is laughter. Then we captives are all at it, collecting palm leaves that have fallen or those they've cut and not used for their own shelter. We weave them in. It's not perfect, but it's pretty damn good for a first effort and I think that concentrating on the activity does something to lift our spirits. The second shelter takes half the time and there's even a feeling of pride when the leader, Rafael, passes each of them and says, '*No está mal. No está mal.*'

'Pah,' says Maria through puckered lips.

It's not the time to speak of luck, yet even in this terrible situation I think we are lucky with our fellow captives. Both are practical and calm in the circumstances and I think Louise could be a companion for Martin through whatever we must endure. We take some comfort in that.

Day Three

Today our mood darkens. We've nothing to occupy ourselves, so sit in the green shadows, overseen by the silent watchers. They're each so different. Miguel is a giant of a man, dark as teak with intense eyes. El Taino – he sounds his name out for us, almost like a challenge (*Ta-ee-no*) – is small and lithe, his skin almost bronze in the sunlight. Two of the fingers of his right hand are twisted and stiff from some old injury. He carries his hand across his chest, so his damaged fingers are impossible to miss.

We're trying to work out why we're in this mess. The Deschamps received the same embassy advice as we did. They too were told that unrest is reported in isolated parts of the island, mostly in the mountain regions. But the tourist centres are heavily protected and the National Parks contain no dangers. The insurgents, in short, we were told, are interested in government installations, 'not a bunch of tourists'.

Jacques and Melanie have been more thorough. He consulted the Internet, but much the same advice was posted there: 'No viable reason why tourists should not enjoy a holiday with a difference on the small but enchanting island of Santa Clara.'

'"Holiday with a difference",' groans Melanie, and it's the first time that any of us has smiled since our capture.

'So why are we here? What can they want with us?' Carol asks. 'I mean, what good can we be to them?'

'Well, what I know,' says Melanie, 'is that the guerrillas want rid of General Quitano – head honcho, *El Presidente*. He started out as a reformer, a champion of the people, but his government's now mired in corruption and he's desperately clinging to power.'

'Impressive,' I say.

'*The Trip of a Lifetime*, according to the ad,' says Melanie. 'I at least wanted to read about where I was going.'

'And,' says Jacques, 'clinging to power means being up America's backside and taking the tourist dollar.'

'So that's what all this is about,' I say.

'Am I missing something here?' says Melanie.

'Well, it's obvious – it's an attack on the tourist

dollar. There's no surer way to cripple the island economy than to show it's not safe for tourists any more.'

'Yep,' says Melanie, 'and while we're on it, no surer way to draw attention to human rights abuses than to kidnap a few rich westerners.'

'But what's wrong with the tourist dollar? I thought they were all desperate for it,' says Louise.

'Right,' says Jacques, 'but that's only because their own money's next to useless. How many times have you had a *peso* note in your hand since we got here?'

'Will they kill us?' asks Martin. The sudden question sends a chill through our discussion. For a moment I don't know what to say—

Martin raised himself up and turned to face the small mirror on his bedroom wall.

'Will they kill us?' he asked it. And again, '*Will* they kill us?'

Taxi Driver. It was one of his father's favourite films. Robert De Niro, isolated and crazed, turning to a mirror again and again: 'You talkin' to me? You talkin' to *me*?' Of course, Martin couldn't match De Niro's intensity – there was still too much of the boy's softness in his adolescent face – so there was a slight unsteadiness in his voice as he held his own gaze.

As he read, he could see himself so clearly, huddled in the green margins of the diary, bent over a tin plate of rice or listening to the sense others were attempting to make of what was happening to them. All the time he'd wanted to be different; to be lithe, to be able to flow up hillsides without panting, to trim a branch without sweat running into his eyes. Instead he'd found himself to be the owner of a large, ungainly body that constantly betrayed him. There were times when he felt the only power he had was to will invisibility upon himself. But there were other times, like this one, when he needed to hear his own voice – the silence which followed it, the concern on his father's face – needed to feel his own words rolling from his mouth like four single beads. And he needed to hear himself again within these white walls, to be sure he had been there and would be again, as far as his imagination would let him.

'Will they kill us?' asks Martin. The sudden question sends a chill through our discussion. For a moment I don't know what to say and am grateful for Jacques, who fills the gap.

'I think no,' he says. 'Think how your shin was bandaged so quickly. It's as live tourists we're of value to them. The only thing is, the longer they keep us, the more valuable we are.' Then he adds, 'For a time anyway.'

'But,' says Louise, 'the government and the Americans – they'll come for us. Won't they, Dad?'

'They'll certainly try,' says Jacques.

There's a silence then and Rafael, who's been standing a little way off, staring out over the hillside, turns to us slowly.

'Your analysis of the situation is not far from the truth.' We stare at him in astonishment.

'Ah, yes, I can speak English well enough. Maria too. El Taino knows a few words. Only Miguel cannot understand your language.' He's smiling slightly as he speaks, enjoying our bewilderment.

'You see, at the start there is much to think of and much tension in the air – yes? – and it is better if we do not speak. Too many questions. Too many questions. Better leave it all to Eduardo.'

'A boy?' says Melanie.

'Eduardo the guerrilla,' Rafael shoots back. 'Perhaps you should know that Eduardo's parents were both "disappeared" by Quitano's illegal government. He may look still a boy to your eyes, but there is a guerrilla's iron in his heart.'

'So, *will* you kill us?' asks Martin, looking straight at Rafael.

'We do not want to have to. It is as this man says. You are of value to us alive. We have let the government know that we have taken this action to draw attention to the abuse of human rights caused by nickel mining in the north. When there is an international commission set up and announced on national television, you will be released.'

'And what would this commission be asked to do?' I ask.

'The government issued licences to United Nickel for mine exploitation without consulting the local people. It is against international law. People have been forced to abandon homes, schools and crops to make way for mining operations that devastate the land. A commission would make sure the authorities protected and guaranteed the rights of the local people and perhaps even suspend the licences.'

'But,' says Jacques, 'no government will be held to ransom like that.'

'We shall see,' says Rafael. 'We shall see. What is your work, Señor Jacques?'

'I work in the oil industry. I'm a diver.'

'Ah, then you will know how much a global corporation like United Nickel cares for small domestic politics. For them everything is a trade-off. They will go along with whatever keeps the field workable and the market steady. A commission will be a small price to pay for that.'

'And if the commission goes heavily against United Nickel?'

'Then they pay their dues and, like a shark, go off somewhere else, where the feeding is better.'

'Meanwhile,' says Melanie, 'with the possible suspension of mining and the uncertainty about tourism, you'll have brought Quitano's government to its knees.'

'Which is where it belongs,' says Rafael.

'This is a very dangerous game you're playing,' says Jacques.

'Oh, I don't care for the analogy of "game", but if you will call it that, yes, we know it. We know we are – how you say? – putting our head in the lion's den, but rather that, I think, than "up its backside". Yes?' No one feels free to share his humour; then he himself becomes serious.

'Oh, do not fear, Quitano's henchmen, and the Americans, and the Mafia who run the big hotels, they'll all be coming for you. But first they must find you.'

'You can't . . . We'll find a way . . .' says Louise, though I thought we made it clear to Martin and her that we mustn't say anything that might provoke them.

'Please, *señorita*,' says Rafael, making calming motions with the flats of his hands, 'and please to all of you, you are right, the stakes are very high, and this is only the beginning. But if any of you do anything to endanger this mission, be clear that we will not hesitate to kill you.'

He looks at each of us in turn. His brown eyes are both serious and sad. But I do not doubt him and hope none of the others is stupid enough to do so.

'*Buenas noches*,' he says and begins to withdraw to the outer rim of our area. Carol runs after him before I can do anything. He turns, his hand on his gun, and for a moment I'm terrified of what she is doing.

'Nick? Nick? Our boy, Nick?' Carol has Rafael by the arm and we see him shrug her off. I've tried not to mention him for her sake, but of course it's Nick who's been filling all her silences. 'Please,' she says. 'Please.'

Rafael places both hands on her shoulders and turns her firmly back towards us. She tells me later that Rafael nodded and smiled and that Nick must be all right, mustn't he?

When did darkness fall? By the time she's returned to us, Rafael is a black silhouette of a man and a machine gun against a starlit sky.

Day Four

How wrong I was about a permanent encampment. This morning we're told to dismantle our shelters and kick our ashes into the earth. There must be a clear plan they're following, for today would have been a good day to stay put. Even as we take to the trail, the sky is leaden, the air moist.

And when it rains, it isn't a tropical five minutes, but for much of the day. At its worst, we cluster under the thickest trees as the rain drums above us. But mostly we walk through it, till our clothes stick to us with water and sweat. We slip on the treacherous paths, and even the smallest river, swollen with rain, becomes a challenge.

At the first of these, we bend down to remove our trainers; but Miguel shakes his head at us, so we tramp across the river-floor fully shod. The mud around the river is a rich, dark red and I note Melanie stepping in it as much as she can, leaving red trainer prints up the riverbank.

'*Por favor, señora,*' says Rafael, almost sadly, and signals to Miguel to brush the footprints away.

'Well, we've got to do something,' Melanie snaps at me.

'Yes,' says Jacques, answering for me. 'You heard them, we've got to keep *tranquilos*.' I'm thankful Jacques seems to see things my way. Melanie has lots of spirit, but she could cause problems for us all.

You'd think the rain would make us feel less alienated from this landscape, but I think the opposite is true. Even in the rain, I feel the heat gathering under my arms, down the small of my back, my waist, my crotch. The heat spots are most intense wherever my backpack touches. Louise winds her hair round her fist and knots it up, but I see a heat rash already forming down the back of her neck. All of us have red marks where our T-shirts and shorts chafe.

When the rain stops, we look across yet another

valley and see the forest stretching out, its trees in the distance like smoke. Everywhere feels like nowhere.

Even Jacques, the strongest of us, seems cowed as we make camp tonight. He leads us in the making of the shelter well enough, but there's little energy about his movements and at times I worry his wielding of the machete is so loose he'll damage himself. For the first time I sense that it is not only guns we have to fear, for we're a sorry-looking bunch. The red mud marks our legs and our clothes where we've fallen. Our faces are haggard with exhaustion. Neither Martin nor Louise asks anything of us. And neither do our captors trouble us tonight. We spoon up our mess of rice and beans, stare into our tin plates and topple into sleep.

Day Five

We sit under our shelter to keep the sun off. Our captors too seem lost in their own thoughts; perhaps like us they're exhausted from the previous days. I write up this diary to stave off feelings of helplessness, a black lethargy I fear will swallow us all.

Day Six

Carol has terrible diarrhoea. All through the night she gets up and goes as far into the forest as she dares. But it can't only be me who's had to listen to it pouring out of her – the sound of exhaustion, stress and the little she's eaten. As she slumps back down beside me, I can see by the shards of moonlight that make it through the thatch the indignity and shame she feels. She simply shakes her head at me, as if the spirit's going out of her. I'm grateful Martin's slept through it all.

This morning at dawn she says to me, 'Look, I don't know if I can . . . these cramps . . .' Then she spots Eduardo approaching.

'Oh, God, no, the boy . . .'

'Rafael wishes to say we rest here for another day. Tomorrow we go for a swim.' Eduardo says it as if it's a gift he's offering us.

'A swim! Oh, Christ!' says Carol and she bends into her cramps.

'Look,' says Melanie, 'I used to be a nurse once upon a time. Anything I have that could help you is back at the hotel, but I know you need to drink lots of liquids.'

Carol groans. But just then Maria approaches with

a mug of hot greenish liquid. Carol swills it around; bits of leaf float in it.

'Drink,' says Maria. 'It will help your stomach.'

Carol holds the mug out in an ironic toast – a way of avoiding her natural inclination to thank – and begins to sip.

'If this kills me, I'll put in a good word for you all.' It sounds more like something Melanie would say, but I know she's trying hard not to be beaten. Still, I worry about the effect of such comments on Martin, who seems more withdrawn, closer to the edge, than Louise. I just hope she can help to pull him through.

For most of the day we rest and sleep.

Day Seven

Eduardo, El Taino and Miguel take us back down the forest path to the river. It doesn't seem so far when it's not raining, and today we carry only what we need. We're led downstream to a small waterfall, at the foot of which is a deep pool in a curved arm of rock.

'Here you can swim,' Eduardo tells us. 'There' – pointing to a ledge of rock edging into the river –

'you can wash clothes.' Within moments he strips to his underwear and jumps into the pool. He surfaces and gives his head a shake, the way I've seen dolphins do, seeing us all standing looking down at him.

'What's wrong?' he calls. 'Don't you like water?'

It's the kind of cocky question I expect from Eduardo. I like his false amiability less and less: even though he's just a boy, he too holds the power of life and death over each of us.

'No,' says Louise, 'not that. I want to know what might be in there. What's dangerous – snakes, insects, animals?'

'Oh no,' Eduardo calls, 'there's nothing like that here. No danger to you but the spikes on the trees.'

We've seen them, black and strong as nails, like a warning to us to keep on the path, not to think there's any way for us through the forest.

Miguel looks at Martin's shin, the redness around the closed wound. He shakes his head.

'You no swimming,' says El Taino.

The rest of us look at each other and decide, Yes, we like water. For a whole hour we almost forget our situation. As Miguel and El Taino sit on the river-bank, their guns on their knees, we have clothes to clean – the water reddening with the dried earth – sweat marks to be removed, hair to be washed. We use the overnight bars of soap we brought with us sparingly – we don't know how long they must last us. Martin not joining us is the one disappointment of the afternoon. Whenever I wave up at him, he's sitting on his heels and holding his ankles, as if he's trying to fold himself away.

After a while Miguel and El Taino take turns to bathe. Miguel seems as shy as we have been when he takes off his shirt. He dives in and turns through the water a few times, but it's only when he's climbing out that we see his back – the startling white lacerations that scar it. On the bank, his reservations gone, he stares us down with fierce, defiant eyes.

I write while Jacques prepares our fire. We've lasted a week and no harm has come to us. There must now be outside forces concerned for us and acting on our behalf. The first horror is past and more and more I feel we're becoming a unit, one that's getting the measure of its captors.

'You know,' says Carol, 'I think that green sludge worked. I could eat.'

Rice and beans again, with some fried plantain this time, but after the exercise and the washing – in clean underwear at last – it actually tastes good, sweet and nutty.

'So, you're a nurse,' says Carol.

'Was – or will be again,' says Melanie. 'It's complicated.'

'Well, we've not got anything else planned this evening,' says Carol.

'Oh, Lord.' Melanie glances at Jacques and takes a deep breath. 'We met in Bali . . .'

'Exotic,' I say.

'Yeah, well, anyway . . . Jacques was working on a rig in the Indian Ocean and I'd just finished my nurse's training.'

'So you *are* a nurse,' says Carol.

'Not quite. Bali was to be my last hurrah before I started work. A gap two months—'

'That turned into a gap sixteen years,' adds Jacques with a smile.

'Aha,' says Carol.

'You guessed it. I got pregnant. We got married and Jacques, my Bali boyfriend, was rarely there.'

'Oh, Mel, don't start all that *never* business again.'

'Did I say "never"? I said "rarely". Argue with that and you'll get a cooking pot on your head.'

Jacques puts up his hands in surrender.

'Sixteen years bringing up baby,' I say, and the minute I say it I know it's a stupid thing to have said, but still I'm surprised by the way Louise turns her narrowed eyes on me.

'No,' she says firmly. 'More like a bird in a cage.'

'Baby, you're all I had,' says Melanie.

'Harrumph,' says Louise, and there's a moment of awkward silence. I'm aware Martin has turned slightly away from me in a sign of teenage solidarity.

'And all the time, I admit it,' says Jacques, 'I am in these exotic places.'

'No, your life didn't change one bit,' says Melanie.

'Oh come on, Mel, Colorado is not the worst place in the world to live a life.'

'Yee-ha!' says Louise and slaps her thigh. 'Cowboy country!'

'Besides,' Jacques says, 'as I tell you many times, it is one thing to holiday in a place and another to work there. Then you do not think of places as exotic – any more than this is exotic. I mean, not very like the posters, is it?'

'The difference between being tourists and prisoners, I suppose,' says Carol, and the thought briefly sucks our hard-won contentment from us.

'Anyway,' says Jacques, 'I say to them both, when Louise is sixteen we'll go on an adventure together. This is it, but not quite as we planned.'

'And if we get out of this—'

'*When* we get out of this, *chérie* . . .'

'All right, when we get out of this, I'm going on a refresher course and I'm going to take the nursing profession by storm.'

'At last,' says Louise.

'Oh, honey, don't be so gloomy.'

'Huh,' says Louise and looks up at Martin as if she's expecting something from him.

'And you?' says Melanie. 'What's your story?'

'English teacher in a high school in London,' I say, pointing at myself, 'and social worker,' pointing at Carol.

'And writer?' says Jacques. 'You always seem to be writing.'

I tell him that yes, it's always been important to me, though I've had little published as yet. 'But still, you know, we try to live the creative life – my writing, and Carol – she draws.'

'And Martin?' says Melanie.

'Has still to declare himself,' I say and we all laugh. 'Isn't that right, Martin?'

'Yeah, that's about right,' says Martin.

'You know what's really weird?' says Melanie.

'Surprise me,' says Louise.

'I know they're there, in the darkness, with their guns and everything. But sitting here with the fire glowing and the talk, it's like this is just a . . .'

'. . . regular campfire?' says Louise.

'Yeah, honey, something like that.'

'Mom, you're going crazy.'

'Nick – you know,' says Carol, her voice breaking, 'our son Nick – he would have loved this.'

CAPTIVES 2
A GAME TO THE DEATH

Day Eight

We break camp and walk into the forest. Any excitement it might once have had for us is long gone. It has become only this narrow trail and on either side a mesh of impenetrable green. It's malicious with it – not only is there the tree with the black sharp spikes, many others seem to have needles hidden in them somewhere, if not on the trunks, then on the edges of the leaves, like hooks, or running down their centres. Whoever thought this could possibly be Eden was greatly mistaken.

Our spirits are affected by the sheer repetitive drudgery of our situation. Louise puts a good face on it – such a good face, it's obviously a source of irritation to Melanie.

'It's not a holiday camp, honey.'

'No, but turning it into a hell isn't the best way of dealing with it.'

'Turning it into a hell?' Melanie shoots back. 'Where have you been?'

'Oh, I was with the Young Pioneers last night, singing songs round the campfire. Didn't I see you there?'

'Oh, Louise, go to hell.'

'Moth-er!'

We are following the same pattern – elusively successful so far, I suppose, for our captors – in that today we leave the cooler air of the hills behind and dip once more into the heat of the valley. But I sense we're walking deeper into it than we've been since the day of our capture. There's an unmistakable tension in the air. Though Rafael hides it well, I note Miguel and El Taino have brought their guns down from their shoulders and carry them in the crooks of their arms.

A scream rips through the air. Miguel turns his gun to us and we drop to the ground as we've been told to. I'm aware of them on either side of us, the slap of hands on metal. But when I look up, there is Rafael, still standing at the head of the trail, a smile on his lips.

'*Tranquilos*,' says Miguel. '*No pasa nada. Miren*.' And to our side, a lithe black piglet scampers through the trees to catch up with its mother.

The trees thin out and we see on a rise a small wooden hut with a palm-thatched roof and a veranda. There's a patch of garden before it, showing green shoots in furrowed rows. An old woman with tight curls of silver hair rocks in a chair on the veranda. She rises when Rafael approaches, her heavy breasts pulling at her grey singlet. She greets him warmly – a kiss on each cheek – and peers over his shoulder at us, nodding slightly as she does so. Of course, I think, Rafael knows them all! He has scouted out his route beforehand and is not behaving from instinct, but from meticulous planning.

Rafael turns to Maria, smiling broadly. 'Handsome but deadly' is Melanie's description. He zigzags his hands a couple of times through the air. I pick out the word *montañas*. They all laugh a little, but I know it's the laughter of release.

'This is good,' says Eduardo. 'This is good for tonight. We all eat well.'

'Well there's a change,' says Melanie.

'Yes, tonight,' says Rafael, 'you are our guests.'

'Guests are usually free to leave,' says Melanie bitterly.

'Ah, that I'm afraid we cannot arrange. Not yet. But it is the time, I think, for a photograph.'

'Oh, Happy Campers now,' says Louise.

'Please,' says Rafael and points to where he wants us to be.

'Close, please.'

Miguel pushes us with the flat of his gun and we bunch up – Jacques, Melanie and me at the back; Carol, Louise and Martin squatting before us. Rafael takes a small camera from his pocket. It's one of the disposable ones – the ones that in all the adverts are only for holiday or party snaps.

'Smile,' says Rafael.

'Yeah, sure,' says Martin.

'Tennes-*see*,' says Louise.

'And again,' says Rafael.

'*Naturellement*,' says Jacques.

'*Naturellement – quoi?*' says Melanie.

'Low tech,' says Jacques. 'Everything is low tech. No radios, no mobiles, no laptops – nothing that could give any photo-sensitive imaging of where we might be.'

'So primitivism is the new sophistication,' I say.

'*Exactement*. The camera will be dropped off somewhere, maybe taken to the city and delivered to the world anonymously, leaving no trail.'

'Oh my God,' says Carol. 'We really are lost, aren't we?'

'Leave it, Mum,' says Martin. He speaks so rarely

these days, Carol looks at him as if she's been scalded.

We sit under the veranda, guarded by Miguel, watching El Taino and the old woman make the fire. But before they light it, they make a spit and cover the whole thing with an awning of woven palm leaves. Rafael appears with a piglet, its throat cut, still dripping blood. A stick is sharpened and forced up its back passage and out of its mouth.

'You learn, eh?' says El Taino, smiling.

'Aw, Jesus,' says Louise.

'Lost your appetite, honey?' says Melanie.

'You're kidding,' says Louise. 'If I could eat a horse, I'm not going to turn up my nose at bacon.'

'Well said,' I say. 'What do you say to that, Martin? You hungry?'

'I'm up for it.'

'Good boy.'

As El Taino turns the piglet on the spit, the first smell of burned hair fills the air and smoke thickens in the V of the awning. Again, it seems without us noticing it, darkness has fallen. We are staring at the red-hot embers when I catch sight of two shadowy figures leaving the shack and moving swiftly down the trail.

'Now,' says Maria, 'better you all inside.' We move into the shack and the old woman, Julia, lights a kerosene lamp. It shows her rusted metal bed. A table. A chair. A chest of drawers. A cross on the wall. The fire has burned through the skin of the pig and the smell of roasting meat is almost overpowering.

'What's happening now?' says Louise, and the way she says it sounds just as if she's at home on any Saturday night when the parents haven't filled her in on their agenda.

'What do you mean, what's happening?' says Maria. 'We wait. That's what's happening. We wait for the pig to cook.'

'And for Rafael and Miguel?' says Jacques. 'I saw them go off down the trail.'

'So you saw what you saw,' says Maria and runs her hand tiredly through her short hair.

'Why do you hate us so much?' says Martin, in that way he has of suddenly springing the awkward question.

'Martin, not helpful,' I say, under my breath.

'I don't understand what you mean by "not helpful",' Maria says. 'But no, is a good question, why I hate you so much.'

It seems for a moment as if she won't answer the question, will simply leave it hanging in the air for us to work out for ourselves. She undoes a shirt button and massages the back of her neck. Then she begins, in an even voice.

'I don't hate you. What are you? Fathers, mothers, two childrens on holiday. No, I don't hate you. I hate what you stand for. Not tourism. I am proud of my country. I want to share it with others. Our people share their history and their pain and their struggle. We are used to sharing. No, I hate the dollars economy you bring, which makes our *pesos*, our once proud *pesos* – now defaced with Quitano's ugly face all over them – almost worthless.'

'We were right,' says Melanie.

'Right?' says Maria. 'You think you're *muy listos* – very clever – to see what is wrong with my country? You look past the beach and the hotel and what do you see? A people with its nose in the dirt. So do not feel too clever, my friends.'

Julia, who surely can't understand a word of this, still nods her head in support of Maria – who isn't finished with us yet.

'And with your dollars you bring prostitution,

thieving, the lack of pride that says, "Why work? I can beg dollars from the tourists." You tourist men' – she looks from Jacques to me – 'you all think we're "up for it", as you say. I've seen it in all your eyes – even in the eyes of the innocent. Yes, it begins and they cannot stop their imaginations going to that possibility. It is so close, yes, no further than their wallets. And how do you think this makes our men feel – our boys – when they see old men with fifteen-year-old girls – girls who should be with them at the cinema? I tell you, it strips them of their dignity, as surely as the women are stripped of theirs.'

'But these are choices,' says Melanie.

'Choices! Ah, your American choices. You say they have choices. At four dollars a month? When doctors have to cycle rickshaws to make ends meet? You call this a choice?' She shakes her head. 'No, no, my friends, this' – and she taps her gun – '*this* is a choice.'

We sit silent, motionless, in the dim yellow light of the hut. A large moth bangs repeatedly against the casing of the lamp till the heat withers its wings. It lies on its back, kicking its legs, till Julia brushes it from the table. She takes out some dried brown leaves from a drawstring bag. We watch as she uses her two fists to crush and roll them together. She places them in the groove of a piece of wood and begins to tease out a whole leaf on the table. It's elastic as skin. She takes the crushed leaves and rolls her cigar, feeling for unevenness, repacking or adding bits of leaf till she's wholly satisfied. She cuts a crescent from another leaf and licks it, smoothing it round one end, then, with a knife, neatly trims the other. She places the first cigar to the side and begins to work on a second.

'No need for that trip to the cigar factory now,' says Melanie.

'Pah,' says Maria.

'Do you know . . . do any of you know' – Jacques speaks into the silence – 'what you're risking with this kidnap?'

'Ay-ee, you think we're childrens playing a game?'

'No, but—'

'Ah, *la vida*. You're asking me if we know we risk our lives? You ask me if I know what life is worth?' She seems amused by the question. 'Do you?' This she issues as a challenge. 'In that moment when you must decide, when you must truly know the worth of your own life? What would you be prepared to put in the scales against your life?' She looks at us each in turn. 'Eh? Eh? Eh? Pah!' This time it is like a small, breathy explosion that tilts her whole head. 'Nothing, eh. *Nada por nada*. Which is why your life is weightless, why it drifts without anchor – through the jobs you do not like and the years passing. Yes, I hear you and I ask again, what are you prepared to put your life on the line for? We know. That is the difference between us. We know.'

There's no sound, but the doorway darkens with the figure of Rafael, then Miguel.

'Maria,' Rafael says, and there's a lightness in his voice. She rises at once to go to him.

There are other questions I still want to ask, but we are waved outside. After the hut's smoky glow, the stars are so thick, the sky seems curved with light.

'Let's eat,' says Rafael, and Julia carves great slabs of pork for us – so sweet and juicy I can't remember tasting anything better. Afterwards Julia brings Rafael, Miguel and El Taino their cigars.

Rafael tells us that we are privileged to celebrate with them the *Dia de la Libertad*.

'Yes, you know, once it used to mean something,'

he says. 'Something real to the people.'

'Well, whadda ya friggin know?' says Melanie.

'If you please, ladies,' he says, and one after the other they light their cigars on the embers of the fire.

Day Nine

Whatever news Rafael went down to the village for, it's not news that will free us. We're given some time in the morning to sit in the shade, then we're told to pack our few things and get ready to go.

Julia kisses the guerrillas on each cheek. Very gravely, she takes Eduardo's face between her hands and looks into his eyes.

'*Cuidado, eh?*' she says. She turns to Rafael. '*Cuidado con el niño*.'

Rafael both nods and shrugs his shoulders, and we start climbing once again.

'Did you get what the old woman was saying?' Louise asks me.

'She said, "Take care of the boy."'

'Yeah, sure,' says Melanie. 'May he rot in hell with the rest of them.'

And we fall into silence.

* * *

Martin heard the front door open and his father stamp the cold from his feet. He knew he would soon be up to see him. He shoved the magazines under the covers and reached for his headphones. He pressed the arrowed start button and his head was filled with the raw opening chords of Test Drive's *Guilty As Sin.* He looked up at the black and white poster on his wall of Tony Kurlansky stripped to the waist, his chest glistening and his hair smeared over his face. Martin had found that if he was looking at that image, when the first words of the song were sung in Kurlansky's ravaged voice –

'You can't escape me
You won't let me go
If I was an island
I'd be covered in snow

And if I was a city
I'd rot from within
I won't play the victim
But you're guilty as sin . . .'

he could shut his eyes and the image lived on, the singer twisting and turning to the clear but broken rhythms, as the music welled inside Martin's head, then spread along his nerve-ends, till he felt like an instrument of sound himself.

He didn't hear the bedroom door open and wasn't aware of anyone in the room till his father touched his shoulder. He felt his father's hand, still cold, through his T-shirt.

'Martin.' He saw him mouth his name.

Martin took off the headphones and pressed the stop button.

'How'd I do?' his father asked.

'You did OK.'

'Thanks.'

'Some tough questions.'

His father nodded. 'To be expected.'

'I suppose so.'

'Oh, good news about Mum, wasn't it?' his father said.

'What?'

'Didn't she say?'

'*What*, Dad?'

'A London gallery wants to have an exhibition of her *Captives* drawings – the originals.'

'Wow,' said Martin. Then, to fill the silence: 'I'm happy for her. Really.'

There seemed nothing else to say, yet his father hovered by his bed. Once again Martin wondered what kind of approval his parents wanted from him.

'You're not coming down then?' his father said.

'No, it's late. I'll go to bed soon. Just listening to some music.'

'What?'

Martin knew his father didn't have to ask. The stack of empty CD cases was all Test Drive, ordered over the Net. He could get five of them on his new machine. He'd listened to nothing else since.

'Test Drive,' he said.

'Isn't it time, don't you think, for something else?'

Martin saw Eduardo, stripped to the waist, his body bent into a Test Drive riff –

'I'm a Chicago mobster,
I'm a fairy queen,
I'm each godforsaken place
My guitar's ever been . . .'

Then he saw his body bending again, writhing, as the bullets hit home.

'No, Dad, I don't.'

'Fine,' his father said and reached out a hand to –

to what? – to ruffle his hair? Was he serious? Martin turned his head away before the gesture could be determined, leaving his father's hand to fall awkwardly on his shoulder.

'Night, Dad.'

'Goodnight, Martin.'

His father turned away in that defeated fashion, his shoulders slumped. But that would have to be the way of it. It wasn't Martin who had stirred it all up again. The memories. They had lived too closely, shared intimacies no teenager should share with his parents. They knew too much about each other – though not the one thing that might have led to an understanding. Let them reach out to Nick. After all, it had been what they'd wanted to do all along.

Martin lifted the covers, brought out the magazines and began to read again. There were times, he felt, for all the re-workings, when his father simply lost control of the narrative. It became repetitive, dull, as his father's eye had grown jaundiced and tired. This next section was a case in point. For three days they'd climbed back up the foothills again and then higher, till, once more, they were astride the valley. It was three days' walking and the diary dutifully recorded the swollen feet, the sweat rashes, the blisters and the aching muscles. It noted how little their captors carried; how serviceable was their combat gear for the terrain; how they themselves, with their sunhats, T-shirts and expensive trekking gear, began to look faintly ridiculous. But the landscape, as described, remained distant, monochrome, nothing but one shade of green. It wasn't how Martin remembered it. And what would Louise have made of these anaemic descriptions? Louise, with her 'Jesus, Marty, there's a rainbow with seven colours in it and they're all green!' Yeah, just what, he would never know.

Eventually they had come to a stand of palm trees, which gave good cover, but whose undergrowth appeared to have been cleared.

'Here we stay,' Rafael had said.

Day Twelve

It looks like we're to be here for a while. It's the farthest inland we've come, following trails that were at times so narrow we had to draw in our shoulders to avoid the evil-looking black thorns. But now there's relief that, for however long, we don't have to climb for a while. We can all, I think, feel a little energy returning to our tired bodies.

Jacques continues to amaze me. The journey seems to have taken little out of him. I think he and Melanie are happier being active, doing something that takes their minds off the situation they're in. So they take the lead in constructing new shelters for us and in digging the latrines – a luxury! Carol and I help, of course, but again it's better that Martin and Louise are active too, so we tend to take a back seat and let them all get on with it. I've the diary to work on and Carol's begun the sketches she'd once thought would be of innocent landscapes. Our captors don't concern themselves with what we do. But today Rafael takes the diary from my lap, as I'm writing. A feeling of utter panic passes through me. Since the beginning there's been a voice saying, *Write this down, write this down*, and now I feel I'm going to lose it all. But all he does is skim a few pages and throw it lightly back to me.

'Tell the truth,' he says.

'I'm trying.'

Carol's hand isn't quite in with the drawing yet, but somehow that doesn't matter – it gives her pictures a quality of rawness and energy that seems to match the experience. She sketches our camp, its shelters, and us – increasingly ragged as we are. She's even tackled our captors, though her work doesn't meet with Miguel's approval. He grinds his thumb into the faces Carol has drawn of El Taino and himself. Unwittingly, the smudged faces only add to the power of the image – enemies unknown and unknowable. El Taino merely shrugs.

'Is not right for Miguel. But I want to know what El Taino looks like,' he says.

Since then, no one's paid much attention to what we do. And I can see no better way to get through this.

Day Thirteen

The strain is showing on Melanie. Today she explodes at what seems a trivial thing. Louise asked Martin to cut her hair. Maria gave them the scissors. Of course, Martin should have known better, but there's so little for them to do and Louise can, I'm sure, be very persuasive. We are always guarded, but often not in sight of each other, so it must have been behind one of the palm-tree trunks that Martin took the scissors to Louise's hair.

She appears in the main clearing where the shelters are, her reddish hair cropped and spiked.

'Christ, baby, who did that to you?'

Martin's standing behind her, not knowing whether Melanie's joking or not. She's not.

'Was that you? What in hell's name did you think you were doing? The mess you've made of my baby's beautiful hair.'

'Mom, I'm not your "baby" and it was me who asked him. If you want to shout at anyone, shout at me.'

'Good idea,' shouts Melanie. 'Did you never think of consulting me about whether it was a good idea?'

'Never,' says Louise.

'Martin,' Carol begins, 'you'd no right to—'

But Louise doesn't let her finish. 'Oh, come on, Mom, get a life. Where are you – still in some mall with the hairdresser's on the corner? I was coming out in sweat rashes. This is so much more sensible for this place. In fact, I should've had it done before all this even started.'

Louise says this in that way teenagers do – like a challenge to her mother, with that forward lean, so she's almost in Melanie's face. I see Melanie's jaw tighten, but she says nothing, and I'm glad Martin's had the sense to keep quiet, for I'm aware of

Eduardo, on the sidelines as usual, grinning at the confrontation.

I think Melanie's accepted she went over the top about the hair, and actually the cut, though crudely done, suits Louise. She's got strong cheekbones and bright, greenish eyes. Still, the argument, though one-sided, ruffles our day, and for the rest of it we keep to ourselves. We're living on a knife-edge and at times the best thing to do is withdraw into ourselves, to avoid any possible conflict.

Day Fourteen

We eat in the late afternoon – rice and beans, but today supplemented with the tiny roasted carcasses of birds Miguel has netted. We let the scraps of meat almost melt in our mouths and suck on the tiny bones. Later, when we're about to leave the fireside and retreat to the privacy of our shelters, Rafael waves us back.

'Hey,' he says, '*un regalo*,' and he throws us a pack of cards. 'Play,' he says. 'Play with El Taino and Miguel. It will make the time pass.'

'Play what?' says Melanie, still prickly from yesterday.

'Pinochle,' says Rafael. 'It's easy. Eduardo will explain.'

Eduardo tells us the rules. It's very straightforward – seven cards each and the aim is to get rid of your cards by putting them down, following face value or suit. There are minor sophistications, but that's about it.

'Well,' I say, 'we can't all play. Jacques, why don't you and Melanie go first?'

'*Bonne idée!*' says Jacques. 'Come on, my little cardsharp.'

'Like, snap!' says Melanie.

'Shouldn't parents let their children play first?' says Louise.

'Well, pardon me for being such a terrible parent,' says Melanie, and it's hard to tell how much she means it. 'I stand aside, suitably chastised.'

'You sure, *chérie*?' asks Jacques.

'Is there a choice here? Have I not damaged my daughter enough with my poor parenting?'

'Oh, Mom, *please*,' says Louise and picks up one of the sets of seven cards Miguel has dealt.

It dawns on me that the *regalo* – present – is not really for us, but for El Taino and Miguel. Since they have taken us captive, their concentration has not wavered. While the others have held their private discussions, El Taino and Miguel have kept their watch on us. Even when we get up in the night, if we must, there is always one or the other of them, the darkest shadow, sitting in the clearing.

Carol, Martin, Melanie and I gather round the players, and although we are only watching it seems the most exciting spectacle. To see how each card is fated to follow another is almost miraculous. The fall into a predictable universe is so calming that the shock when a penalty card – a two or a king – is played, and then another on top of it, is almost unbearable.

'*Merde*,' says Jacques and slowly picks up his four extra cards. I note him grimacing across at El Taino, who has two cards left. Jacques sits forward on his haunches, as if ready to spring. El Taino puts down a ten of spades, then an ace of hearts, and holds up his empty palms.

'Hold on, what was that?'

'Ah,' says Eduardo from the shadows. 'I should have told you. The ten allows you to play another card and the ace, remember, you can play anytime.'

'Great game, when you find out the rules after the event,' says Jacques.

'Well, move aside,' I say. 'Let the professionals in.' But I can see Jacques is not amused.

'No,' he says. 'I'm not finished here yet.'

'I am,' says Louise and makes way for Melanie.

El Taino and Miguel clink tin mugs of coconut milk and another hand is dealt. Once we get the hang of it, it's a quick game, though everyone shows patience with Melanie, who ponders all her options.

'I'm thinking,' she says. 'I'm thinking.'

'Jesus, Mom,' says Louise. 'It's a game of chance. Just play something.'

Still, in any game of chance, chance will dump on someone, and in this sequence of games it's Jacques who is suffering most. His concentration has intensified with his losing streak. His eyes are narrowed on the small patch of ground where the cards are laid. He squints at them in the fading light.

Opposite him, El Taino and Miguel have become limpid. They put their cards down in extravagant sweeps compared to Jacques, whose hand flicks out like a snake's tongue. Often El Taino and Miguel look at each other and laugh at their good fortune.

Miguel plays his king of hearts and turns to Melanie.

'Huh,' she says and places the king of clubs on top of it.

'*Ai-ai-ai*,' says El Taino, pretending to reach out for the pack to pick up his penalty cards. Jacques visibly relaxes. Then El Taino, with his two stiff fingers, plucks a card – a king of spades – and lays it down on the other two kings.

'Fuck it,' says Jacques, throwing down his hand and standing up. 'I've had it with this.'

Miguel's smile gleams. '*Qué mala suerte, hermano*,' he says, and El Taino gives a little giggle.

'What's that? What's that he said?' says Jacques.

'Dad, calm down,' says Louise.

'I will, once I find out what that big ape's saying to me.' Jacques says this as he stands over Miguel. A frown has crossed Miguel's face – all the lightness gone from it. He stands up with some difficulty, as Jacques refuses to give way before him.

'*Qué te pasa?*' says Miguel and pushes Jacques in the chest.

'Who are you to push me? I'm sick of being pushed around!' Jacques' is the loudest voice we've heard in two weeks. He returns Miguel's push with interest. What happens next I have to play back in my mind, it happens so fast. Miguel's knees appear to buckle momentarily, but he is only reaching for a machete propped behind the palm log he was sitting on. He brings it up in one movement and drives the wooden handle into Jacques' stomach. Jacques' eyes widen as the breath leaves him and he jack-knifes in pain. But Jacques isn't left to cough and splutter, for Miguel goes down on one knee beside him, seizes his hair and pulls back his head. He holds the blade of the machete to Jacques' throat. We think of the dog, the pig . . .

Rafael steps forward from the darkness.

'*Basta!*' he says and waves Miguel away. El Taino puts an arm around Miguel's shoulders and leads him off.

'Now, *señor*, you will be calm.' He addresses Jacques, who is still on his knees, still retching in pain and fear. 'Remember what you were told. You are our prisoners. If you put in danger what we do or make it difficult for us, we will not hesitate to kill you. And wouldn't it be a pity to die for such a small thing as a "big ape" telling you that you had *mala suerte* – bad luck?'

There is not another word spoken by anyone as we make our way to the shelters, Melanie holding Jacques by the arm, Louise following behind. In the darkness, I'm sure I hear him sob.

CAPTIVES 3
A GLIMMER OF HOPE

Day Fifteen

Jacques doesn't come out of his shelter all day. Melanie tells us that he's in pain and passing blood. But I think worse than anything for him must be the shame. Melanie glares at any of our captors who come near her. She makes a comment to Rafael about the damage his 'muscle' has done.

'What is the meaning of "muscle"?' says Rafael.

'Oh, come on,' says Melanie. 'Your henchmen, your hard men, your thugs.'

'*Cálmese, señora*. Yes, Miguel and El Taino are *hard* men. The times have made them hard. And Miguel was too rough with your Jacques. I have told him. He knows the importance of discipline. But we have always been a violent society – ruled by the dog, the whip, the machine gun. You cannot expect such men always to turn the other cheek. And, *señora* – please, I'm still speaking – when you talk of "muscle" and "thugs" and so on, you do not know of what you speak. You have much to learn and, until you do, it is better – like the boy Martin, I think – to listen and not to be so quick to judge.

Remember, nothing you say will stop us from doing what we have to do.'

'"From doing what we have to do." You heard what he said,' Melanie repeats for Carol and me. 'Doing – what – we – have – to – do.' She stabs each word into the silence.

'God,' says Carol, reading the unspoken. 'You heard him last night too – they "will not hesitate to kill us". These were his exact words. *Will not hesitate*.'

'Calm down, Carol. Why would they kill us? We're no good to them as *dead* hostages,' I say.

'Don't use that word "hostages"! Have I not said, don't use that word? It carries too many echoes . . . too many echoes of Iraq. Have you forgotten what happens to hostages there? Their white pleading faces. And for what? To be slaughtered like animals. Laugh if you want, but I saw what Miguel did to that dog. And I can't look at him splitting open coconuts without thinking of skulls.'

'No one's laughing, Mum,' Martin says. But Carol pays him no attention.

'"We will not hesitate . . ." You heard him.'

'Look, love,' I say, 'it's not a comparable situation.'

'No? How?'

'Because those hostages were made to plead for the impossible. No government's going to change its policies for a bunch of fanatics.'

'Well, isn't that what they're asking *their* government to do?'

'No, and they're not a bunch of Che Guevaras calling for *Revolution or Death* either, as far as I can tell. This lot's dumping on tourism and they're asking a mining company to treat its workers and the environment with some respect. Which side would you be on?'

'I can't believe you said that!'

'What?'

'That they're in the right. Those who took us at gunpoint and hold us against our will and will not – in their own words – hesitate to kill us. Have you lost your mind?'

'No, I'm just trying to hold on to some sense of perspective.'

'*Perspective*. *Perspective*. Oh, my God, I'm never going to see Nick again.'

'. . . never going to see Nick again.' It was the sound his mother made that Martin remembered. Woven through the words was something like a high-pitched wail, almost beyond the human ear. But not beyond Martin's. And he'd heard this trapped sound most frequently when she said something his father – for the clarity of the narrative perhaps – had chosen not to include in the diary. 'Oh, Lord, I can't bear to lose him for a second time, not just when we've got him back.' Nick, of course.

But his mother hadn't been wrong to think about the shelf life they had as valuable hostages. For each week the guerrillas maintained this situation, they added to the success of their mission, though they must be wary of overplaying their hand. News media were fickle, and once hostages faded from view, so too did their worth. Who really knew when such a time would come?

Although both parties had to share the incredible boredom his father's diaries couldn't quite capture – the repetitive elasticity of each day; the sitting around; the distastefulness of unwanted intimacy; the constant pangs of hunger and thirst – for the guerrillas it was bearable because time had a purpose. For the captives, each one of them had to find a way of dealing with despair and a home-sickness that was graver than words could catch.

Martin recalled his father telling his mother that he didn't think it prudent for her to let Jacques catch sight of the sketch she had done of him, buckled over, with Miguel, machete raised – an artistic licence – above him. Sometimes it was better, he explained, not to see ourselves as others have seen us. Yes – Martin smiled – better to be the author of our own histories.

And so Martin carried on reading of how, in his father's eyes – with its lethargy, its discomfort and its humiliations – time passed.

Day Twenty

Strange things are happening to us. I write with a passion I thought had left me for ever, Carol draws compulsively and I find reams of poetry I thought I'd forgotten returning to me. It's mostly of the rhyming kind. I resurrect it in my head – each verse is a loom with missing parts, but I find that if I can remember a few end words, I can weave the rest. It becomes something, I hope, to keep us amused. So I find myself, in our jungle theatre, as the sun goes down, declaiming *Morte d'Arthur* by Alfred, Lord Tennyson, to the other captives. As a student I recited it for drinks in the bar, but I haven't done it for almost thirty years. It's a sonorous piece and I've been rehearsing it in my head for days, yet still I'm surprised by how the words move me. Perhaps it's simply tiredness that brings emotion so close to the surface. But I can tell, out of the corner of my eye, that my captors' ears are drawn to the rhythm.

'For what are men better than sheep or goats
That nourish a blind life within the brain,
If, knowing God, they lift not hands of prayer
Both for themselves and those
who call them friend?'

'Repeat, *por favor*.' It's Rafael's voice and he draws closer to catch the words. I recite them for him. 'Again,' he says, as if there's an urgency about what the words may say. Now he says them with me. His slight uncertainties, the awareness that he is shining a light on the words inside his head before he says them, slow down my usual delivery. I speak the lines as if for the first time.

'For what are men better than sheep or goats . . .
If knowing God, they lift not hands of prayer
Both for themselves and those
who call them friend?'

'Pah,' says Maria. 'Impressive, but "hands of prayer" will not clear corruption from our land.'

Rafael nods sadly. 'You have something to say?' he asks.

'I'm amazed,' I say. 'These lines, you speak them . . . like a poet.'

'Yes, I was a poet once.'

'And still you are,' says Maria with a shake of her head, as if it's a weakness.

'So, how did you go from a love of words to a love of guns?' asks Melanie.

Rafael smiles at her. 'A brave question, *señora*, and it deserves a longer answer than I can give now . . . At first my allegiance to the cause was not political, but simply cultural. I wanted to write poems in my language which addressed the history of my people. All of the history. All of the people.'

'But cultural allegiance is not enough,' says Maria, and she turns to Rafael as she says it, as if this is a conversation she has had with him many times.

'No,' says Rafael. 'And that is what I learned from Maria. She always recognized the necessity of the political dimension.' Briefly he turns to her. 'You see, she is the strong one.'

'And you,' says Maria, 'you are still talking as a student.'

'Still,' says Melanie, 'you have chosen a strange route for a poet.'

'Not so strange,' says Rafael. 'And remember I said I *was* a poet. But anyway, what is poetry about but imagination? No, Miguel and El Taino are not literary men. But do you know the imagination it takes to see a new world, to hold it before your eyes? Yes, and to keep it there, even as your face is being ground down in the dust? Listen to me. You have been to the *palacio* in the capital, yes? You have seen on your fine tour the cases full of the symbols of power – the swords, the plumed hats, the medals awarded in all the wars of suppression. One day, my friends, we shall have a museum like that in every town. In it will be the shirts of men and women like Miguel and El Taino. There will also be photographs, yes, of what Quitano's henchmen have done to them. You have seen Miguel's back, yes? And the instruments of torture will also be there, but they will be behind glass and speaking like so many accusing tongues of the cruelty of what has been. The scars on Miguel's back – that is the map we follow, that is the symbol of our struggle.'

'This "we",' I say; 'who is this "we"?'

'Do you not listen?' says Maria. 'It is the people, those who can never be blindfolded, silenced, defeated.'

'Yes,' says Rafael, 'it is first of all them. Then it is the whole country and its history. We honour the living and the dead in our struggle.' He turns and gives Maria a gesture somewhere between a wave and a salute. Maria watches him go.

'You love him, don't you?' says Melanie. The air grows strained as the question hangs there.

Maria turns her face stonily to her. '*Love*, you say? There are things greater than the individual heart. We meet, you know, as privileged white students. Rafael, he has hair that falls everywhere and it's the colour, you know, of molasses. And everywhere he goes he is speaking poetry. As natural as breathing. But I see unhappiness in his eyes. I know he needs more – for himself as much as for his people. So we work, Rafael and I, and the love, the love becomes no more personal, no more selfish. It embraces the sufferings of Miguel too, and El Taino and all who want to see a better future. So, no, we do not share any more that "in love" thing you like so much. The struggle is about feelings that are stronger and deeper. What can you know?'

But Melanie nods an understanding that is tinged with sadness. 'I'm tired,' she says. 'Goodnight, Maria.'

'Goodnight.'

Day Twenty-one

A day of surprises! We have a visitor. Miguel brings him in, his arm round his shoulder, both of them grinning. It's the guide from Island Adventure, the small worried-looking young man with the jaundiced skin. It's clear that the climb up here has exhausted him. After each laugh he stops and puts his hands to his sides to take deep breaths.

'Slimy bastard,' says Melanie.

'Can't disagree with you there,' says Carol.

'Eduardo,' says Rafael, and Eduardo stands back to watch over us, while they gather round the guide. The young man wipes sweat from his forehead with the back of his hand, then lifts a satchel over his damp T-shirt. He pulls a newspaper from it. Rafael grabs it. His hands tremble as he reads. Then he passes the paper to Maria with a smile.

'Ah,' says Eduardo. 'Gabriel has delivered the papers.'

'Huh, Gabriel – yes, I remember. So what *good news* does he bring us?' says Jacques.

'You will soon know.'

'And Gabriel, how did you persuade him to join you?' I ask.

'That is a question you do not have to ask if you have eyes and ears in this country.'

For a moment I'm reminded of one of my most arrogant pupils, who talks back without any thought or deference to me. Rafael leaves their group and comes over to us with the newspaper in his hand.

'You see,' he says, 'there you are.' It is the photograph of us taken at Julia's on the front page of *La Corriente*, the daily paper. 'It says, *Fears for Tourist Hostages Grow*.'

'Great,' says Melanie.

'Yes,' says Rafael, 'it's good. Very good. It also says that tourist numbers go down and there is fear for the dollar.'

'But nothing of what you really want,' says Jacques.

'Oh, I say half. They will begin to feel the pressure now.'

'I want to believe you,' says Melanie, 'but falling tourist numbers is one thing; getting Quitano to change his mind is quite another, isn't it?'

'Yes,' says Carol. 'You can't know how he's going to react.'

'Oh, I think we can. We know our enemy,' says Maria, who has joined us. She glances at Rafael. 'For, you see, General Quitano is Rafael's uncle.'

Martin remembered the first jolt of the revelation – the astonishment on all their faces – and once again he was baffled by how his father had arrived at his editing decisions. At every stage, every word, the diary opened up great vistas inside his own head that it didn't explore. Moments that cried out for expansion, explanation – more colour than either his father or his editor seemed to favour. Many of these memories Martin held back – not allowing them to surface, not till he was ready: not till he could control the truths that must come out. But here at least he thought his father might have fleshed out rather more of what they learned from Rafael that night about the main protagonist in this whole affair – the one who was making everything else happen . . .

* * *

General Quitano began as a good man, they had been told, a well-meaning and educated man. When he took over government, after the years of instability, he had appeared almost reluctant to accept power. But he promised he would make everything *calmado* again. The workers would go back to work, the land would yield, the *peso* would be trusted to hold its value once again.

It was in the first optimistic days of power that Quitano, pleading the desperation of inexperience, persuaded his brother Abel, Rafael's father, to leave the city university, where he was a professor of philosophy, to become his Minister of Education. Abel took to the post like it was his mission. '*Education is the key*' was his mantra. He criss-crossed the countryside, talking to teachers, to local bureaucrats, to parents and to children about his vision for the future – a land of educational opportunity for all.

But then he'd sit with a smattering of uniformed generals and dull-suited yea-sayers around a shining oval table in the oak-panelled room of the Government Palace, and his requests for finance, for changes to the educational requirements for all children, would be stalled, overruled or consigned to the oblivion of the next meeting.

'Yes,' Quitano once said, putting his arm round Abel's shoulders at the end of one more budgetary freeze, 'I know how close these changes are to your heart, but let us remember what the first duty of government is – to establish stability and the rule of law.' Then he'd leaned his head towards Abel and hissed, 'There is still dissent in the land. It cannot be tolerated.'

'But what has that to do with education?' said Abel.

'Ah, my dear innocent, there is a choice – teachers or policemen. We keep the children locked up in school all day or we control insurrection in our streets. And I think,' he said, smiling, 'we have very happy children.'

'Yes,' said Abel, 'and most of them are begging.'

'Abel, remember who you are talking to!' said Quitano, his face clouding.

Martin remembered how Rafael's handsome face had responded to the story he was telling. How his face had darkened at Quitano's threats; and how, when he said, 'Education is the key,' Maria had nodded to herself: '*Sí, la educación es la clave.*'

There were many times when Abel wished to tender his resignation, but who would then speak for the children? Who would then trumpet, '*Education is the key*'? Certainly none of the other gentlemen sitting around the table. New medals seemed to grow on their chests at each meeting; their cars grew longer, sleeker; their mistresses – minor starlets – more bejewelled. Haciendas began to spread on the outskirts of the city, behind high walls and electric fences. Soon no one knew in which one Quitano lived; he moved like a medieval monarch around his palaces.

'Here,' Quitano said to Abel one day, 'here is a present from the government.' It was the keys to an estate on the far side of the island.

'No,' said Abel, who had just seen his budget increase by a miserable two million *pesos*. 'I cannot accept.'

'Oh, come on. This is not the people's money. No one is taking it from your precious education.'

'Well, where . . . ?'

'From friends of this government.'

'And who are they?'

'United Nickel. Yes, a big American company is our friend. Our best friend, Abel. Our best friend for a future.'

'Yours, I think.'

'Do not dare to accuse me.' Quitano's voice echoed down the corridor.

All this time, of course, Rafael was enjoying a privileged lifestyle. But it wasn't enough to blinker him to the poverty, illiteracy and lack of opportunities that lay outside the hacienda's walls. And what he did not see, Maria gave him eyes to see, so the lines of his poetry became cleaner and sharper. He had freed himself of his family name, preferring instead to publish under his mother's name, Portuondo. Perhaps, he thought, well-chosen words would be able to cut through the tangled mesh of interests that bound his father.

Rafael and Maria were not the only ones to see how Abel had aged in his ministry and how betrayal was beginning to show in his eyes: how genuinely sorry he seemed to be that he could make nothing happen. Yet still he travelled through the countryside; still he spoke with passion – and with apology – to teachers, parents, children and to community leaders. Often his wife, Mercedes, accompanied him now. She had been a teacher herself once and, whereas teachers and parents could admire the fervent belief Abel had for his cause, children loved

Mercedes for the unaffected warmth of her concern. 'You should be the politician!' Abel said to her more than once.

Word began to spread of a good man trussed up in a corrupt situation.

But word also spread to Quitano's sharp ears of this paragon who was gaining popular support. Worse, that his ponce of a son, Rafael – 'The ungrateful wretch who casts off the family name as if it is something to throw in the gutter!' – was involved in student politics and that Abel was making no effort to curb his enthusiasm. The universities, he thought, needed watching more closely.

But Abel was not the innocent Quitano took him to be. He was aware of the danger he was in and would have been careless if it were a danger he faced on his own. Putting his family in danger was another matter entirely. He made arrangements for his wife to leave the country for the safety of Miami. It was ostensibly a holiday, but Quitano's contacts told him of the long-term lease taken on a property. It was the excuse he wanted. He had Abel arrested on charges of corruption and political intrigue – that should tarnish the troublesome saint. Word reached Rafael that he and Maria should immediately

go into hiding. He dropped his literature studies . . .

There is a silence after Rafael has spoken while we try to come to terms with this fresh information. Maria lays a hand briefly on Rafael's shoulder, but her face is expressionless.

'So, is your father still in prison?' I say at last.

'Shot "while trying to escape",' says Rafael. 'A typical Quitano cliché.'

'But this man, Quitano,' says Melanie, 'he'll never agree to anything. Oh, shit, we're screwed.'

'Ah,' says Rafael. 'He wants to hold onto power above anything. If the US put him under pressure, he may not be such a good friend to United Nickel. Those mining licences would dry up or even be withdrawn.'

'So the Americans could eventually be *your* friends, eh?' says Melanie.

'The world,' Rafael answers, 'is a complicated place. And this "game", as you call it, is held in a delicate balance.'

'Yeah, our lives, you mean, hanging by a thread,' says Melanie.

'I hope not,' says Rafael, 'but we will see, yes?'

* * *

'So *how* will you kill us?' Martin looked straight into the mirror. It was the brazen way he wished he could have looked into Rafael's eyes at that moment. It had been the question uppermost in his mind. But it was the one he had not dared to ask.

CAPTIVES 4
THE BLOODY END

Day Twenty-two

Bit by bit, we find out more and more about our captors. They're good stories they tell, but we must remember, no matter how they present their case to us, that we're being held here at gunpoint and that the threat of death hangs over us every day. Still, what's strange is how much, at times, they're prepared to reveal to us – Rafael's background, for instance. It's no surprise to find out it was a privileged one – though it's still hard to follow the journey he made from student poet to revolutionary. But if we get out of this, identifying him will be very straightforward. This morning I ask him, 'Now we know all about you, don't you fear what will happen to you once all this is over? *If* you plan to release us . . .'

'I have always said that is my wish, if circumstances permit it. For the other matter, I have friends. Your concern is touching, but needless. And remember, this is merely a skirmish – a call, if you wish, to all who are oppressed by Quitano and his puppet-masters. It awaits an answer.'

* * *

Of them all, it is Eduardo who remains most distant from us. He keeps on the edge of things – a dark, shadowy figure. Since the first interpreting he did for Rafael, we've had little to do with him. Even so, too often I see him hanging around Louise, if ever she's trying to find what passes for privacy in these circumstances. She smiles uncomfortably and I sense her unease in his presence.

Not surprisingly, Jacques and Melanie worry about her and about what advantage may be taken of her. For this reason they take comfort, as we do, in the growing friendship between Louise and Martin. Though he says nothing, you can tell by his mood that he thrives in her company, that he pretends to be casual when Eduardo is around – threesomes are hard enough to negotiate, but when one of the three is armed and dangerous, well, my heart goes out to the boy. I know Carol's does too, but we do better, I think, not to dwell on what lies so close to our hearts – powerlessness only weakens us further.

These are not ordinary times we're living through. Carol and I, Jacques and Melanie have each other. Why should Louise and Martin not support each other too? And why should we, as parents, not turn a blind eye to matters that in normal circumstances we might have some say in? If it helps them to spend time in a shelter of their own, I can see no problem with that. Still, there's an uncomfortable moment when Jacques learns what's afoot.

'Louise . . .' he says, and his jaw clenches. Even beneath his tan you can see his face flush. There's a moment when we half expect the return of the old Jacques, but he simply turns and heads for his shelter.

There was a knock at the door, then it squeezed open a crack.

Nick stood in the doorway, darkening it. Since Martin had been in captivity, it was as if Nick had filled all his space. Martin returned to school to find Nick had become like a mascot to his friends, a favourite of teachers who congratulated themselves on his 'progress'.

'Can I come in?' said Nick.

'Door's open.'

Nick was eight months older than the boy who'd watched the back end of a lorry kick up dust and seen the rest of his family severed from him. He was almost as tall as Martin now, but had grown like a sapling that has overshot itself. Hair that had once been cropped short had grown and, gelled into careful disarray, it made him appear softer, somehow younger, than he'd looked the year before.

'What d'you think then?' Nick asked.

''Bout what?'

'Dad on TV.'

'Oh that. He didn't lose a leg.'

'Eh?'

'He didn't make a fool of himself. He looked OK.'

'Think it was OK about the French people?'

'Yeah – uh – look, I don't know. It was a long time ago, for Christ's sake. It's over.'

'OK, it's over.'

'Yeah . . .'

'Mum says it might snow.'

'Oh, yeah.'

'But Dad says it's too cold for snow.'

'Exciting. Place your bets.'

Nick smiled.

'So what film did you watch?' asked Martin.

'Something set in the future – about a family.'

'Sensitive or violent?'

'Mum chose it.'

'Ah. Subtitled or not?'

'Not.'

'Sounds good.'

'Mmm, wasn't really.'

'Tough shit.'

'Goodnight then.'

'Yeah, goodnight.'

But Nick hung around the door frame – why did people do that with him? When it's time to go, for God's sake, go.

Then, 'Goodnight,' Nick said again and closed the door behind him.

Sometime, Martin thought, he would get around to asking Nick what it had really been like for him – from the moment when that blur of a face had peered into the taxi, seen an old couple and a child and dismissed them with a curt wave. The lorry. The dust. The silence. The media attention back home, the gentle questioning from all those government agency people and then the long limbo of hope. Ask him, like, in a real conversation. Till now it had been easier just to tell Nick what everyone had tried to tell *him*. 'It's over, Martin. It's over – we're back – we're safe – we're lucky – we can move on – put it behind us. It's *over*.'

And it almost had been, till the fuss over the diaries. But the story they told – the story that engaged him now – clearly was not the story he had to tell himself. For months, that had been gnawing in the pit of his stomach and it didn't let him think about anything else.

Day Twenty-three

Contact with the outside world! We haven't been forgotten. There's a distant thrum that breaks our forest silence. You can't hear a bird or the buzz of an insect any more. The helicopter's only the size of a dragonfly when we first see it at the head of the valley. Miguel and El Taino force us into our shelters. Their agitation is clear when Miguel thrusts his barrel into Jacques' back.

'Hey,' says Jacques. 'Easy, eh?'

After the days up here more or less 'rubbing along', it's an uncomfortable shock to be so harshly treated again. But we all remain calm – though I think each of our hearts beats with expectation.

'Not long now,' I say. 'Not long. They'll find us.'

'Do not be so sure,' says Jacques, and true enough, looking into the stillness of the clearing, I see that the shelters are barely visible. The palms show a brief flurry of activity, then the helicopter veers off and continues to climb. The silence that reasserts itself is more imposing than before. It leaves us gasping for air.

'What now?' says Carol.

'Nothing,' I say. 'Best just stay till they call us out.'

'They're looking for us,' says Melanie later. 'Glory be. We're gonna get out of this hellhole.'

'That helicopter's certainly spooked them,' I say. 'Look.'

Out in the centre of the clearing an argument is taking place. Rafael is pointing up at the distant mountains, but Gabriel, our deceitful guide, shakes his head and points in the other direction, down towards the coast.

'You see how alike Gabriel and El Taino are,' says Melanie. 'The same sallow skin, the same cheekbones. They could be cousins.'

'Maybe *mulattos*,' I tell her. 'You know, mixed black and white blood.'

'You don't have to tell me what a *mulatto* is. I'm American, remember. One thing I know about is race.' She glares at me and I wonder whether civility among us can last much longer.

Gabriel's holding both hands before him and, in a

shunting motion, gesturing fiercely. Eventually Rafael nods and claps him on the shoulder. Gabriel's triumph is marked only by a muted half-smile.

'Pack everything. Fill in latrines,' says Eduardo. 'Tomorrow, early, we leave.'

'For the coast?' says Melanie.

'Perhaps,' says Eduardo. Then he gives Louise one of those looks that have aroused all our suspicions. I wonder if he knows that the endgame is in sight and he has little time to make his move. One more reason we're happy Louise and Martin have each other.

Day Twenty-four

For much of the night it has rained. We rise in darkness. We gather up our belongings as Miguel and El Taino take their machetes to the shelters, scattering thatch and supports. There is no cause for speech and the tasks are carried out in silence – a numb silence, for it seems strange to be leaving this spot after the time we've spent here. I wonder where we are in this ordeal and what our journey to the coast will bring. By the time we're ready to go, the black cut-outs of the palms are already dark green.

* * *

We walk till almost midday. We clear the thickest of the forest canopy and the sun is strong on our backs. But Carol in particular is struggling. She falls, twists her ankle and limps on in pain.

'We can't go on like this,' I say to Rafael. 'We must rest for a bit.'

'After the river. We cross first and then we rest.'

We take the steep slope down into the river valley. I give Carol all the support I can. Rainfall has swollen the river, and it rushes and twists down the hillside. On the river plain you can see where its force has taken great half-moons of red earth from its banking.

Rafael shouts ahead to Gabriel, who nods affirmatively and waves his hand further on. Finally we come to a part where the river spreads into a broad shallow weir. It still flows strongly here, but close below its plaited surface there's a line of stepping stones. Just beyond these, the river tumbles into a deep pool, then sweeps on down towards the coast. Gabriel nods: This is it.

Miguel places one boot on the first stone and draws the other foot across. The water washes over the ankles of his boots. He stretches a boot to the next stone. At the same time he reaches out a hand to one of us. To our surprise and dismay, it's Martin who reacts first. Their eyes lock together. As Martin stands on the first stone, Miguel steps onto the second one. Whether its edge is rounded or whether Miguel simply miscalculates the manoeuvre, he twists as he attempts to regain his balance and his left leg seems to hang in the air momentarily, before the force of the water tips him over and he falls backwards into the river. His pack hits the water first and his head whips back and strikes one of the stones. There's a burst of blood in the water, before the strong current carries him away like a log down into the deeper reaches of the river.

'Martin!' Carol's first thought is for Martin, who stands statuesque on the first stone, his arms curled around himself. I reach out to him and with locked fingertips pull him to the safety of the bank.

But Carol's shout is embedded in El Taino's shout for Miguel. Now Rafael and Eduardo hold him back, talking fiercely to him all the while. The whites of his eyes roll, and he casts Rafael and Eduardo from him as if they were bindings of straw and leaps down the riverbank after Miguel's body.

We collapse on the grass. Martin allows himself to be held awkwardly in Carol's arms. She strokes his forehead over and over again.

'Martin. Martin. Martin.'

After a while El Taino returns, shaking his head, his eyes glistening. Rafael is first to rise to greet him. He says a few words and lays his hand on El Taino's shoulder. Gabriel approaches and seems to shrug an apology. For a moment I think El Taino will take his machete to him. But the energy and the anger have left him. He buckles to the ground, his head between his knees; his broken fingers held like a flag above one shoulder.

We improvize a camp near the river. Rafael wants us to stay here for as long as we can to retrieve Miguel's body.

Day Twenty-seven

After two days of searching, Eduardo and El Taino find Miguel's body, lodged between two rocks, and bring it back up to camp. They're exhausted. The body is grey as slate and wrinkled. River crabs have been nibbling at the softened flesh – small ragged wounds. His proud face is bruised and swollen, beaten up like an old fighter's. But even in death we're slightly nervous about looking at him, face to face, for long.

El Taino and Jacques have scrabbled in the earth and dug a shallow grave. Rafael stands at its head and insists we all join him. Once again Jacques humiliates himself, stubbornly sitting with his back to us all as we gather round the grave. El Taino pushes his muzzle hard into Jacques' neck.

'Stand, *señor*, stand. All stand for Miguel.' His voice shakes.

Melanie screams, 'Jacques, stand, for God's sake!'

Rafael places his hand on El Taino's forearm. He lowers the gun and Jacques slowly rises to his feet.

'I dig the man's grave. Must I honour him too?' he mutters to me. There's a minute of silence, till Rafael speaks, first in Spanish, then in English for us all.

'No matter where death surprises us, let it be welcome. And let other hands pick up our weapons where they fall. One day, Miguel, you will hear other men come forward to intone your funeral dirge till the air rings with cries, not of grief, but of victory. For wherever a life is lost, however it is lost, it is a life lost in battle. It is a gift for a cause greater than any of us . . .

'Miguel, comrade, soldier of freedom, we salute you.'

So Maria was right. Rafael's still a poet when he wants to be. We stamp the earth down on the unmarked grave till it's flat and hard and Rafael's sure not even the wild pigs could root Miguel out.

Day Twenty-eight

In the time of our waiting, the river has become more easily passable. We cross by the stepping stones that cost Miguel his life and soon we're glimpsing the shining blade of the sea through a fringe of coastal palms. We pass only one poor hut on our journey and now must be far from the town. I think of the first shacks we passed at the start of this ordeal. It is with the same casual '*Hola*' that we're greeted now by an old man. Rafael exchanges a few words with him. It seems we'll have fish to eat tonight.

It's late afternoon and the sun is just beginning to lay itself across the water – the closer we are to it, the more beautiful a deep blue it becomes.

After the claustrophobia of the forest – always on narrow paths, always with a thick canopy above us – you can see how each of us visibly changes. Our shoulders come down; we lift up our faces and breathe in the air. We walk along the narrow strip of beach re-connecting with the world at our feet. Everything is like a message – shells, seeds, even the plastic detritus from a world we were once so keen to escape. Our captors are out of place here in their heavy fatigues with their machine guns slung over their shoulders. Only El Taino seems unchanged, his taut face a reminder of his loss and of the threat that still hangs over us.

Rafael stops and removes his bag, throwing it on the ground and arching his back.

'Thank God,' says Melanie. 'Well, at least they've brought us to the ocean.'

'A day at the seaside,' says Martin glumly.

'Oh, come on, Marty,' says Louise, and Martin brightens a little at that. 'Isn't it great to get out of the forest? Do you think they'll let us swim?'

'I ask for you,' says Eduardo, in that oily way of his. He has words with Rafael and comes back nodding.

'Great! Come on, Marty, let's go!'

They're just like any other young couple on the beach. They strip down to their underwear and take to the water. We're all close behind. We turn in the water, weightless after so much physical effort.

As we swim, El Taino collects firewood, and soon a small fire is burning and the old man's fish is cooking. Rafael himself dishes it out to us with some plantain on broad shiny leaves.

As the sun begins its rapid sinking, Rafael removes his shabby uniform and walks down to the water.

'Maria,' he calls, 'a swim.'

'You go,' she says, and to El Taino, 'And you too, Taino.'

El Taino lifts his shirt over his head and turns slowly to Gabriel – the first time he has looked at him since Miguel's death. But Gabriel shakes his head, like someone with a fear of water.

Louise gets up. 'Well, I'm for a last evening dip. Anyone else?'

'I'll go,' says Eduardo.

'What about you, Martin?' Carol asks.

'No, I'm fine.'

I feel irritation, wondering how Martin can let Eduardo get away with it.

Maria never takes her eyes from Rafael as he wades into the water. Above him, I note, a lone cloud touches the edge of the moon like blotting paper. It's the last thing I can be clear about. The rest I must piece together as well as I can.

* * *

Martin had always known this was where he was heading, but when he arrived, the words started to swim before his eyes. Their letters meshed into barbed, impenetrable bushes. His memory supplied flashes of gunfire; shouts. An occasional phrase, sometimes a whole sentence, surfaced from the darkness –

'Hit the sand!' –

and Martin knew that hiding there somewhere in the undergrowth of words was the famous description of how Eduardo, in an act of desperation, made a grab for Louise to protect his own precious skin. How they threshed in the water, one against the other.

And how, after the shooting, there was silence. Boots. Sobbing. The curtness of an order.

He wiped his eyes and read his father's last words:

When the shooting stops, Carol crawls over the sand towards Martin and pulls him back into her lap. He lies in her arms, his body limp, his eyes wide with shock. We stay like that – the three of us – till two soldiers come to us over bands of broken shells, their weapons still held in readiness. An American voice asks, 'You OK, buddy? This your family? It's all over, folks. You'll be home real soon.'

Outside, the street was glazed with ice. *Too cold for snow.* Long ago he had heard the hall lights click off. The length of the long dark avenue, his was the only lit window. He turned Test Drive up as loudly as he could. Kurlansky snarled –

> *'What will it take to make you whole?*
> *What will it take to give you a soul?*
> *We're twisted, twisted in isolation . . .'*

The last word was drawn out, jarring as a train crash. But the music could not quell the final images conjured from the words of his father's diary. Tears of grief and injustice tracked down the magazine's last page. So many details left hanging, so much unexplained. At the first gunfire, Gabriel had run towards the National Defence Force troops and their American advisers, waving his arms.

'I wasn't to know he didn't carry a gun,' said the soldier who reportedly brought him down. But there was a death more innocent than his.

Martin couldn't remember when he'd started

pencilling notes in the margins of the articles. Certainly it had been after everyone had gone to bed. But once he had started, he found he couldn't stop. He'd pulled his desk light closer to the paper and found that, with a tiny spidery handwriting, he could write between the lines.

The first flakes began to fall sometime in the early hours of the day, like blossom from the dark, laden sky. By the time the first light shone between the curtains, and he heard the cars revving through the thick snow, he knew he had the bones of a story he would write one day. He could almost feel it now, fleshing out inside his head.

PART TWO
A SECRET RIVER

CHAPTER ONE

don't you like water?

It was as if someone had pushed the vegetation back to reveal clear water cupped in the heart of the forest. To Louise the pool had the intimacy of a secret.

Miguel and El Taino sat on the rim above it with their guns resting on their knees. Eduardo stripped down to his underpants and dived like a knife into the water. He surfaced and called up to them.

'Come on in. Cool down.'

The hostages all looked at each other uneasily and Miguel gestured that, Martin apart, they must go in the water.

'Come on. You see, you must,' Eduardo shouted again.

Louise noted how the light that filtered through the trees above made his hair shine like wet coal.

'What?' said Carol. 'They expect us just to . . . ?'

'Well,' said Jacques, rolling his broad shoulders, 'that water does look inviting and–'

'Easy for you to say,' said Carol. 'You're not the one with three men staring at you.'

'Three?' said Jacques.

'Eduardo, Miguel and El Taino.'

'Don't we count?' said Tony.

'You know what?' said Melanie. 'I don't care any more. I need a wash and this looks like the best bet yet.'

'Right on!' said Louise and lifted her T-shirt over her head.

She felt a sudden excitement, the kind of excitement that makes you clumsy taking off your clothes when you're in a race to be first in the pool or the ocean – all fingers and thumbs. But this wasn't the pool or the beach. This was a waterhole in the middle of the jungle, God knew where. In phys. ed. changing rooms, when there were only girls present, Louise turned her back on everyone and curled her shoulders round breasts she feared might be too large – already becoming her mother's daughter. Yet here she was, in front of a bunch of people who'd kidnapped her and threatened her life, just lifting her T-shirt off and stepping out of her shorts. She noted that Carol at least was still in her mental changing room, but the others were taking off their clothes less carefully and folding them roughly into small piles.

Then the awkwardness came.

If she'd been able to strip and dive straight into the clear water, it would have been fine; but she found herself instead poised on the lip of the bank, her arms instinctively crossed over her bra, seized by a fresh panic.

Around her, she heard the forest titter.

Eduardo grinned and beckoned her in. His skin was light brown – like caramels. 'What's wrong? Don't you like water?'

'It's not that . . .' said Louise.

'Don't worry,' Eduardo called. 'There's nothing in the water that could harm you. We have no water snakes.'

'How disappointing,' said Jacques, as Louise hit the water and felt its coolness envelop her. She was soon aware of other, larger bodies beside her. Occasionally an arm or a leg would brush against her; a spray of water momentarily blinded her. But mostly she turned in the water, curled in on herself, and felt the water support her and grant her a temporary freedom.

'Aren't you coming in then?' she called to Martin, who had edged himself down the banking, past the point where Eduardo had said they could wash their clothes.

'They won't allow me,' said Martin. 'Because of my leg.'

'Poor you,' Louise called and ducked under the surface again.

Louise had not been alone in finding some escape in the water that day. The other hostages too had returned refreshed, more able to confront their situation. There was an openness about their conversation that night that suggested bonds would be formed to get them through this. It was Martin, who'd been unable to lose himself in the water but had remained on the bank feeling ungainly and excluded, who was most burdened by what he had seen there.

The least of his discomforts was seeing the dark coins of Melanie's nipples through the wet gauze of her bra; the greatest seeing Miguel's back, crossed with grooves of white hot ash. But it was neither of these images – nor of the otherworldly beauty of a blue bird hovering over the water – that haunted him in nights to come. Rather it was a line of fine gold hairs in the small of Louise's back. The sun had picked it out as he'd crouched behind her on the edge of the bank and it pricked all his waking dreams.

CHAPTER TWO

a flower in her hair

From the start of their captivity there had been a rule: no talking on the trail. At times this intensified their discomfort. Louise could see the nervousness in Carol rise whenever anything brushed against her. The green trail was to her a gauntlet; one she must run with few words of comfort to allay her suspicions about what might threaten her. Once a fierce hollow knocking caused her to jump.

'*Carpintera*,' said Miguel, turning his fingers into a beak.

'It's a woodpecker, Carol,' said Tony. 'Only a woodpecker.'

'Ah, of course.' Carol nodded tiredly. 'Silly of me.'

Louise played it a different way in those first days. She simply lowered her eyes to the track, to the roots that crossed it, the grit pressed into it, and saw it as little different to the trails she had followed through the Rockies with her parents. It was one of the things weekends were for. To get in the pick-up and leave the sprawling suburbs behind. For lately the city was claiming more and more of the gentle hills around it. The communities appeared almost instantly, with their schools, their malls and their long, gently undulating streets, named after every variation involving *Glen*, *Valley* and *View*. But still it was possible, on a clear day with a high blue sky, to escape them.

Mostly it was the front range of the Rockies they reached. Her father, when he was there, flicked on the four-wheel-drive, and they climbed the twisting logging track to the head of the trail. Like now, she thought, it's just like now. She almost convinced herself that if she were to lift her eyes from the trail, to either side of her would be firs, silvery aspens, juniper, above a floor of pine needles. And ahead, through the trees, she would see not more of the same, but the clear line where the trees had surrendered their advance, and above that line only rocks and the blue-edged distance. Blue. Blue tingeing the tips of the firs; star-shaped blue alpine flowers; blue mountains. And yes, exactly as now, her father striding confidently ahead, making light of the climb; then herself, then her mother obstinately pegging them both back, the explosion of her hair like anger itself.

'Hey, Jacques,' her mother would shout, 'you're away for weeks, then you come back and won't even walk with me.'

Her voice, rasping in the altitude, never reached her father. But it would always strike home with Louise. When she was younger, it seemed that her father's job concerned geography as much as time. *Daddy is going far away.* They looked at a map together, traced a finger round a lit globe. *But Daddy will be thinking of you always, no matter where he is, for you are his precious.* Lately though, until this trip, geography was never mentioned: time was the sole issue.

'How long this time?' her mother would say, and Louise became aware that her mother was as often looking at her when she said it as she was at her father. It was as if it were a question they were asking together.

'A few weeks. Look, we're going away together soon. All right?' There was no talk of 'precious' any more.

Louise kept her eyes down on the trail as long as

she could, sometimes counting out the time – one to five hundred, doubling it, trebling it. But when she looked back up, it wasn't the airy, freeing vistas of the snow-capped Rockies she saw, but the enclosing world of the rain forest. At first she'd felt each green pulse pressing in upon her, as insistent as the guerrillas with their orders and their guns.

'It's all the bloody same, wherever you go,' she heard Tony say up ahead, and Miguel drew the flat of his hand across his own throat as a warning not to speak. But Louise was discovering it was not so. She remembered at school being told that the Inuit had no word for snow. Instead, where others would only see snow, they had two hundred words for every kind of snow you could imagine – hard-packed snow, newly fallen snow, melting snow and so on. It was the same, Louise felt, to say that the forest was 'green'. For there must surely be as many different shades of green as there are kinds of snow. There was the green of a fresh shoot that was so pale it almost seemed to emit light, and there was a green that, before the eclipse of the sun each night, was almost black. And there was every kind of green in between – a green that was almost purple and one that burned as gas does with a blue tinge. And this blue-green was carried through the veins of some leaves; red-green through others. And colour, though it was endlessly variegated, was only the start of it. For there was texture too – the glossy finish of those leaves that were first to turn to black; the fine hairs that coated some leaves; the tiny hooks that protected the stems of others.

It seemed the invention of the forest never tired. There was nowhere the green couldn't reach. Whenever they arrived at the top of a hill and looked ahead, it was green that met their eyes, a smoky, bluish green filling the distance. Even Louise could find this dispiriting.

More often it was what was closest to hand that drew her interest – the hollows, the shadows, the suddenly parted green curtain that revealed one more secret: small purple orchids that attached themselves to tree trunks and glowed like anemones; trailing plants like guy ropes that came down from the trees and rooted themselves in the earth; the extravagant white flowers she'd seen some women wearing in their hair.

She'd never worn a flower in her hair. Back where she came from, girls didn't wear flowers in their hair. She was wondering why that might be, when

Eduardo joined her at a point where the trail opened up. He held out to her a leaf shaped like a spearhead.

'You know,' he said, 'there are at least sixty varieties of mango that grow here.'

'Really?' she said. 'Like I could *care.*'

Eduardo shrugged and fell in behind her again. She began to wonder what the slight flare of her hips looked like to him and to regret she'd fended him off. For there were questions she wanted to ask. She turned round.

'The scars on Miguel's back . . . How did he get them?'

'Sometime,' he said, 'I may tell you.'

But their light voices had carried to Miguel. He gave Louise the same fierce gesture he had earlier given to Tony. When Miguel looked away, Louise passed it on to Eduardo.

CHAPTER THREE

a horse struck by lightning

It seemed they needed a photograph. Miguel and El Taino pushed them into a group and pointed to where each must go. Martin found himself squatting between his mother and Louise. How strange were the intimacies he was being forced to share. Like the other night, when his mother rose more than once from the shelter. He heard the vegetation crack beneath her, almost as if she'd gone no distance at all, then the rush of liquid and wind that poured from her. He'd kept as still as a stick, barely daring to breathe, as she brought her shame back into the shelter and lay between them again.

'Oh God, I think I'm dying,' she whispered.

The first two or three nights he had allowed himself to be held. He was scared: the dark was intense and within it he foresaw the direst consequences for them all. When his mother's thin arms came around him, he bent himself into her, resting his head in the hollow below her collarbone.

'It's all right,' she said. 'It's going to be all right. We're going to be all together again. Aren't we, Tony? We are, aren't we?'

'Yes, course we are.'

All together again.

He couldn't shift that feeling that when she was holding him, she would rather be holding Nick. Nick, her baby. So he began to stiffen slightly when her arms tried to enfold him, to turn away with a '*Mu-um*, I'm just getting comfy.' It seemed perfectly natural in an adolescent boy who was already taller than his mother. Besides, Martin was beginning to adjust to the fact that here, in this situation, they could not protect him, they could not guarantee that everything would be all right. His father couldn't do that. Not even Jacques could do that. So he began to create a shell around himself, to ensure that neither fear nor pity could weaken him. That was why it didn't seem unusual to him when one of his captors addressed him as *hombre.* For strange though it seemed, in one incredible week he began to feel that he was leaving his boyhood behind.

Yet this shell that was forming around him, how thin it was still and how easily breached.

'Tennes-*see*,' said Louise, refusing to be bowed. She turned to Martin, once the camera had clicked, and her outer thigh, naked, lay flat against his.

'Crazy, this,' she said.

'Yeah,' he said, 'isn't it?', his mouth so dry the words would barely come.

They had been told they would eat well that night and they did – a young pig, its roasted flesh pink and sweet – though they'd had to wait for it, penned in an old shack, listening to Maria berate them. After the meal Rafael drew on one of the cigars the old woman had made for Miguel, El Taino and him, the smoke rising in the still air, the ash growing long and white.

The old woman, Julia, told them that once she'd seen a horse struck by lightning. It had turned to ash, white as that ash on Rafael's cigar. But still it had stood there, till she went up and touched it on a star still outlined on its forehead. It was only then that it had crumbled and the last of the storm wind had blown it away.

Yes, said Miguel, he'd heard that could happen.

Eduardo finished the translation and Melanie

wondered aloud why anyone thought they would want to hear such fairy tales.

'So,' said Rafael, 'you do not care to hear our stories. I wonder what you *do* care for, apart from our steady sun and our blue sea. Yet, you know, you are privileged today.'

'You're not serious,' said Melanie.

'Yes, I am. For today, this evening, you have celebrated with us the *Dia de la Libertad*.'

'That's a laugh,' said Melanie.

'*Basta!*' snapped Maria. 'Listen. Learn.'

Miguel edged out of the darkness.

'It is the day,' Rafael continued, 'when we honour our first great liberator, Manuel Grau. It was he who gave his life to drive the Spanish imperialists from our land. It is a day when everyone in Santa Clara should think of freedom and sacrifice.'

Louise narrowed her eyes in thought. She was remembering the threads of a story told on a brief historical tour of the capital. She had been hot and impatient for it all to be over, lingering at the back, as the others had nodded and checked the images on their digital cameras. Manuel Grau sat on a white horse in a plaza in the centre of the city. His arm was raised to his threadbare troops and he would soon be dead. His short life had been lived in smoky rooms as an exile and in brief, inconclusive campaigns that swept the island. If the campaigns were not in his favour, it was not only his soldiers who suffered – villages were fired, collaborators shot. Yet Manuel Grau had been born the privileged son of a wealthy planter. He had chosen this life, the freedom of his people.

'He inspires us still,' said Rafael. 'We just take the war to the oppressors in a different way.'

Louise was still unimpressed. But talk of the *Dia de la Libertad* led her back to her last Fourth of July celebration. It was what you could do here sometimes, to quell the boredom and the strangeness of it all – take something someone had said like a ticket that triggered a memory. Then project it onto the shadows and the stillness of the night.

Their next-door neighbours, the Drakes, had been holding their annual barbecue. Trestle tables were set up in the two-car garage where everyone could lay their predictable offerings. One regular was famous for sauerkraut, another for cookies, and 'Careful of that salsa! If you've not tried it before, go easy. It's got the kick of the devil.'

Neighbours brought chairs and iceboxes, ready to

sit out the day. Most of the kids were younger than Louise these days – a spate of high-school leavers going east to college had left her stranded between generations. Even remembering it now made her feel lonely. Oh, but these kids were cute in their Stars and Stripes T-shirts with their chocolatey mouths. She just stayed on the grass verge, her face turned to the sun, and they came to her every so often to ask her to take them to the rest room or to show her their new sneakers.

The men stood in the drive, talking politics and football. The mothers sat on picnic chairs and told stories about their husbands. *Absence* was Melanie's story, though she buttressed it with humour. Louise was old enough to know that Jacques was envied by the men for his adventurous life and that there were wives whose voices developed a light trill when they looked up at him and asked for a hamburger: 'So, Jacques, how *are* you? Where've you *been*?'

As the heat went from the day, Jim Drake brought out a bag of fireworks and arranged all the smallest seats for the kids to watch from the kerbside. The fireworks were low-key – pyramids that foamed into colour and soon subsided; ones like iridescent spiders that crawled a few dazzling steps and were gone. The children applauded each one.

Then other bags appeared. These fireworks were more sinister. Some emitted great plumes of black smoke. Others fire-cracked across the road. The gloomiest of them simply expanded into black snakes, writhing themselves into ash. Children covered their ears, curled their heads between their knees. It was dark when Dan Morris's pick-up took off to buy more.

He returned with two large bags. He twisted fuses together and fired them with his gas torch. The fireworks exploded in a random sequence, lighting up the darkness of the road.

'There goes thirty dollars, right there,' one of the neighbours said.

Dan Morris held the boxes under his arms, ripped the cellophane off and began to prepare his next explosion.

'Iraq,' Jim Drake said simply. 'His platoon was attacked. He lost his best buddy. Never the same since.'

The roadway was Dan Morris's theatre now and he never left it. He was small and thick-set, and when the fireworks briefly lit up his face, he was wearing a different mask each time – pleasure, pain, nothingness. It was a theatre with no care for its audience and with little sense of celebration. The kids had lost interest – withdrawn up the front lawns or gone inside to watch a video. Sparks from other parties had begun to flare up silently against the black cutouts of the Rockies, as Dan continued to litter the street to the strains of one more country singer's version of *God Bless America.* Something dark was spreading through the heart of the party and no one knew what to do. Not till Jacques, towering over him, took Dan by the arm and led him gently off the road.

Louise thought of that evening again the following morning, when they were about to leave the shack and the cold ashes of the fire. Julia kissed each of the guerrillas in turn, then held Eduardo's face between her palms. Out of respect, Louise imagined, he had not turned away like you might expect a boy to do, but had stayed still as she'd wanted him to. He smiled slightly at the concern in Julia's face.

'*Cuidado, eh,*' she said to Rafael. '*Cuidado con el niño.*'

And there was something vulnerable about Eduardo then that she'd not seen before – or not cared to see, for why should she? *They* carried the guns after all. It was the smiling vulnerability that reminded her of Lance. She'd known him the previous year, when she still held the general opinion that most of the boys her age were geeks, into nothing but computer games and football. Lance had captured her interest – a shadowy figure with floppy black hair, who'd 'gone off the rails', her mother had been told. Mary Steinberg's boy from a first marriage gone wrong. 'Reckon there's Indian blood in there somewhere,' she'd heard someone say.

At the Fourth of July party she remembered him at the margins of the evening, firing his pocketful of tame fireworks for a group of the smallest kids. In school, he'd stayed aloof, challenging teachers, running rough-shod over his fellow pupils' careful hierarchies. Louise liked both the brazenness that scared others off – and the vulnerability. She hoped he saw something of a kindred spirit in her. Whatever, they'd begun to smile at each other and to give each other greetings in the corridors, not in the showy way the geeks did – 'Yo!' 'Hey!' 'High five!' – but simply by raising a hand. Lance's long slim fingers rarely rose above waist height, but his sharp brown eyes always looked directly at hers. Louise had thought that, perhaps over the long summer vacation, they could begin to be friends – or more than. But then, a week after school finished, his mother had packed him off to his father. He'd never come back.

'*Cuidado, eh.*' She liked the sound of the words. '*Cuidado con el niño.*'

CHAPTER FOUR

the failure of friendliness

Gabriel's father seemed to be shrinking into his bed. He held his sides and coughed – a wet, painful cough. Gabriel raised his father's head so that he might expel the spume that threatened to choke him.

In the corner there was the glare of a small TV screen. Gabriel twisted its aerial to try to receive a picture that was more than lines of grey metal filings dancing before his eyes. Finally he managed to still the picture, to give its images hazy outlines.

General Quitano was thundering out his message. Terrorism, he was saying, will never be tolerated in the patria. And he knows, mark his words, that terrorist activity is imported, is fanned by extremists, who are not motivated by love of our island, but instead by hatred of our friends. *Small* people. *Bitter* people.

Quitano has always managed to bring out a crowd,

and this day – the *Dia de la Libertad* – is no exception. They have risen early, those who make up the crowd, and packed into rusting buses or lorries, or simply walked, threatened with losing their jobs, to avoid the heat of the sun. They mass now in the Plaza de la Republica, waving the two small flags with which they've been issued – the Stars and Stripes of the country Quitano insists is their equal partner, and their own flag: the red stripe of blood that has made them, the blue of the sea that surrounds them. But apart from the core around the podium, there seems to be little enthusiasm for Quitano's message. On the fringes, in the shade of trees hung with speakers, they chat or beat out rhythms with the cheap flag-sticks. They let the rhythm pass through them and want, always want, to dance.

'This latest outrage,' said Quitano, 'what is it designed to achieve? I'll tell you. It's the work of our enemies. It's designed to take from us a chance to sit at the top table, to keep us as a nation of peasants and slaves. I ask you, is this the way forward?'

There was a pause, for Quitano was used to speaking without interruption. Now, however, he needed a response.

'I say, is this the way forward?'

'No!' the people roared.

'Is this the life we want?'

'No!' the people roared again.

'Are we to be peasants and slaves?'

'No! No! No!'

And then the spontaneous chant: 'Qui-tan-o. Qui-tan-o. Qui-tan-o.'

At this point Gabriel's mother returned from market, a loaf of bread and some plantain in her string bag.

'*A-ba-jo! A-ba-jo! A-ba-jo!*' she chorused. 'Down with him. Down with him.'

General Quitano eased himself back from the lectern and nodded his head, the wise father of the nation. An upraised palm – it was all it took – silenced the crowd.

'So,' he said quietly, 'it is clear. Those who carry out such actions have no support among the people. And without the support of the people, their little fire will soon go out.'

Gabriel's father was waving his hand furiously at the television: 'Ay no!' Gabriel twisted the aerial, and in mid-breath Quitano was dispersed into a grey fuzz.

'We will see,' said his father. 'We will see whose fire

will soon go out, won't we, my son?' His eyes glittered briefly in his haggard face. 'Come,' he said, 'help me. We will sit outside for a while.'

It took time for Gabriel's father's breathing to steady itself after the exertions of inching out onto the veranda, so they were sitting in silence when they saw the three men approach from the road. One of them was a stranger – a city man in a linen suit, wearing expensive trainers and a baseball cap.

Gabriel glanced at his father, but could not tell whether it was worry etched on his face or simply the pain he always wore.

The other two men Gabriel recognized as Pablo and Raul, the local policemen. They were cousins, and friendless in the town in spite of all their empty greetings. Gabriel could see how puffed up they were now, with their wrap-around sunglasses and gleaming holsters, walking either side of the stranger. Small men, buttressing power.

'*Qué día más lindo*,' said Pablo.

'Isn't it?' replied Raul, as if the beauty of the day were exclusive to themselves. Gabriel's father's eyes drilled into the stranger. He would have nothing to do with the puppets, only their master.

'This is Señor Mason from America,' said Pablo,

lifting his sunglasses to rest on his head. 'He has come all this way to speak to you.'

'*Buenos días,*' said the American. He'd picked up the lingo in Guatemala, dealing with the same kind of shit, the same incompetent policemen. Up close Gabriel could read TEXAS COWBOYS on his baseball cap.

'*Qué quiere conmigo?*' said Gabriel's father in a whisper.

'First,' said the American, 'I'd like you to invite us all inside out of this heat.' He spoke Spanish as if it were brittle – a language so weak-boned it never got out of bed, never knew how to work or how to party or how to dance.

After the strengthening sun, it was dark at first in the wooden house. Mason dabbed his head and squinted around till he caught the looming shape of an armchair.

'Ah.' He sank into it and said to no one in particular, 'You never heard of air con here?'

Gabriel helped his father back onto his bed. His father's eyes were closed and he was breathing heavily. Only Pablo had come inside. Raul sat on the rocker on the veranda, his arms along the rests, his hands hanging loosely. He tipped his head back and rocked.

'These are bad times,' Mason said. 'Bad times around here.'

'You,' spat Gabriel's mother. 'Why do you come around here, telling us of bad times? We do not need you to tell us of bad times.'

'Hey, *tranquilo, señora,*' said Mason, pretending offence. 'Only trying to be friendly.'

'Friendly? We don't need your kind of "friendly" round here.'

'And what kind of friend do you think I am, *señora*?'

'I know. I know you. I know you, United Nickel man.'

'Well, good for you, *señora.* But from where I'm looking, I think your husband there needs all the friends he can get.'

'How dare you come into my house and tell me this? You, who took his land–'

'Gave him a good price, *señora.*'

'A good price? You take his land and you tell him if he wants to eat he must work for United Nickel. A job that gives him the disease that will kill him. You think this is a good price?'

'Now, you know there's no proof of a link between nickel mining and cancer as well as I do.'

'Do I? Do I? Let me tell you the proof I see. I see a

healthy man come home coughing every night. A man who used to work the land all day – sunrise to sunset – a strong man, reduced to an invalid in five years. Do not come into my home to tell me of what I know.'

'I admire a man who can work, *señora,* and I should remind you of the pension that United Nickel is paying your husband – and his family – though it accepts no responsibility for his illness.'

'Four dollars. Four dollars a month. For the loss of his health; the loss of the sacred land he loved; the loss of his dignity.'

At that last, Gabriel's father pushed himself up and held his shaking head as still as he could. He fixed Mason with watery eyes in which, deep down, there was still something polished and sharp.

'Forgive me.' His wife breathed the words with such quietness, only her husband could hear.

Pablo was bending down to look out of the small window at the back of the shack. He could see over the bay to the small isthmus where the tiny airport was, its runway improbably laid over the rise where the land was closest to the sea. That was where he'd picked up Señor Mason. Even as a trouble-shooter for United Nickel, Mason could not quite disguise from Pablo how beautiful he found this place – how blue the sea, the sky, and how fierce the slabs of light on the old colonial battlements. And that dense green mystery that so effectively hid those who had caused his trip.

'Come on then, let's keep moving,' he had said to Pablo. 'Do you love your job? I just *love* my job.'

The usual gaggle of tourists had deplaned with him. *Oohing* and *aahing*. How Pablo hated them, their love of colour, of picturesque poverty. If it weren't for his uniform, he thought, he wouldn't be able to bear living here – a nobody like everyone in this family. But one day that magical strip would launch him far away from this place; one day he'd be a taxi driver in *Nueva York*. He had another cousin there.

'They all drive like you there, Pablo. You'd fit in, no problem.'

He turned from the window. Things didn't seem to be going well.

Mason sighed. The failure of friendliness always disappointed him.

'Let us then touch on the matter that really brings us here. This one concerns your son, Gabriel.'

'My son has nothing to do with United Nickel,' said his mother.

'No indeed,' said Mason. 'But perhaps he has something to do with vanishing tourists.'

'*Cabrón,*' said Gabriel's mother. 'Leave my house, leave my house now, son of a whore.'

It was not the best way, Gabriel's father knew, but all he could do was shake his head, muttering, 'Pilar, Pilar, *por favor* . . .'

'Well,' said Mason, 'it's become obvious we can get nowhere here. Isn't it time *you* did something?'

Pablo stepped forward immediately and as importantly as he could.

'Gabriel Ferrer, I must invite you to come with us to the police station. We have questions we need to ask concerning the abduction of foreign tourists on the island.'

'You do not take him alone,' said his mother. 'I'm coming with you, Gabriel. This is nonsense!'

'No, *señora*. He comes alone. Really, it's better this way.'

'It's all right, Mother. I'll go. I have nothing to fear.'

'We hope not,' said Mason, smiling at Gabriel and his mother.

Gabriel leaned over his father to say goodbye.

'Say nothing,' his father whispered. Gabriel could

feel how light was his father's breath and how the smell of decay came with it.

This time Mason walked ahead, his hat off, testing the heat of the sun. Gabriel was flanked by the cousins. It was a complex thing, Pablo mused, power and how it touched you: you could feel it flowing into you from the weak and the powerless as well as from the strong.

'*Primos!* Cousins!' Gabriel's mother shouted. 'Where is your shame?'

Back inside the house, she knelt before her dying husband and wept into his lap.

CHAPTER FIVE

like all prodigal sons

Martin looked at his father, squatting like a toad over his diary. His father's eyes were narrowed to focus on the tiny writing. His worst fear was the paper running out. Beside him, his mother leaned her small sketchbook on her thighs, her head lifting and lowering as she sketched the shelter and, to its side, Miguel and El Taino leaning against a palm trunk. Every so often she paused to pin her lank hair behind her ears again.

It appeared to Martin that his parents' fear had mostly been replaced by a new intensity that the others saw as distraction, selfishness. They seemed intent on finding a shape for what was happening to them as it was happening; too busy to notice what did not fit a narrative they had already imagined. How else were they to survive?

Any day now, the schools would return. Perhaps

Nick would be one of the returning pupils – getting some normality back into his life. Staying with one of his friends perhaps – an endless sleepover – or with his lawyer uncle, Ralph, and his young wife in the big Georgian house that always made his father so uneasy.

The summer term began with the trees dripping with blossom, the exotic come to suburban streets. His father held the end of another year in sight and seemed more relaxed, more expansive, as he ambled down the corridors – the ones Martin avoided. Even the feud with the headmaster became something he could make light of. 'Yes, Headmaster, I'm sorry the paperwork's late. But look around you. Nature's on the side of the creative. It doesn't need to fill in a form to advance.' He even thought he saw the man smile. Still his mood could be tripped. When there was a beige self-addressed envelope on the carpet, Martin could hear his father sigh before he opened it and his eyes skimmed yet another rejection slip.

'*Not for us! Not for us!* Christ, how anodyne can you get? I mean, what do they bloody want?'

'It's still a good story, Tony. Nothing changes that,' his mother said.

'Doesn't it? Doesn't it really?'

'No. Come on, try somewhere else,' she said, an edge of tiredness in her voice her husband never noticed. 'There are always other magazines.'

So she would dust him down and buck him up. The rejection slips would pile up, clogging his pen, and more and more Martin became aware of his father's dissatisfaction with himself and with his life.

It was also in the blossom-time a year before that two policemen had come to their door with Nick, standing slightly unsteadily, between them. His small, almost shaved head glowed bluishly in the hall light. It wasn't the first time and no more serious than the others: hanging about the playground at night, being rude to passers-by, getting his hands on cider and alcopops. A typical hoodie. But it was the first time that one of the policemen had recognized his mother as the social worker from a case that had involved them both.

'Well, let's hope the young man takes a warning this time,' the policeman had said. 'Next time it won't be so pleasant.'

'Yes, Constable . . .'

'*Sergeant.*'

'Yes, of course, Sergeant. Sorry. Very sorry. Thank you. Sergeant.'

'Can't even look after her own,' she'd heard the sergeant say to the other policeman as they walked to the front gate.

When his father returned home, she was ashen. As Martin listened outside the door, she told him how shame and embarrassment had gripped her. She feared for Nick. For the future. She felt they'd lost him to a set of foul-mouthed shadows on BMX bikes. She'd seen a hundred families fractured in just the same way. Martin saw his father take her in his arms. She shook: a small woman becoming lost in his father's big, shambling body.

No one mentioned a breakdown. It was just that the washing was never done; the meals she had agreed to cook never appeared. Nick was rarely home. All his energy was spent escaping the enormous tiredness that had enveloped his parents and threatened to engulf him too.

She agreed to take leave of absence and began to draw again. 'Something for yourself,' the counsellor had said. But still, the family couldn't shift that exhausted feeling of being on a still-bound ship going nowhere. One evening Martin had heard the soft voices of his father and of Christine, the counsellor, rising up the well of the hall.

'Are you concerned at all about Martin?'

'About Martin? No, not at all. Why do you ask?'

'He's very quiet.'

'Well, that's his nature. He's very different from Nick.'

'I can see that. It's just that he doesn't seem to be very happy.'

'But none of us are with all this business with Nick – and now Carol being unwell.'

'I understand and I know it's not easy for any of you. It's just that, well, maybe Martin's feeling everything more than he's showing. He seems a very sensitive boy.'

'Oh, he is, he is—'

'Look, Tony, all I'm saying is, keep an eye on Martin too.'

'Oh, we will . . . I will. But please don't say anything to Carol. I can't have her worrying about anything else.'

'Of course, Tony.'

'Thank you, Christine. Thank you.' His father shuffled to the door to show her out. Suddenly he'd got old.

Soon after that conversation his father, in an act of desperation, booked the Easter trip of a lifetime. Whether it was in anticipation of that, or whether some confusion he'd been feeling had simply resolved itself on its own, but Nick began to calm down, to stay in, to 'go straight'; to become, like all prodigal sons, *precious.*

'Oh, Martin,' his mother said one day. 'It's a mystery to your father and me, but I think Nick's turned a corner at last.'

'That's good.'

'Oh, isn't it? This trip could be the making of him, you know.'

'Hey, Martin,' Louise called from another part of the clearing. She wanted him to cut her hair with a pair of scissors she'd borrowed from Maria.

'Why not ask her then?' he asked.

'Come on, Martin, do you think she's here to do us favours?'

'Your mum?'

'Get real. Like, Mom thinks we *are* our hair. She'd never do it and I need it done. I just can't bear it up, down or wherever. I want it off. What's your problem?'

'Nothing,' said Martin. 'I'll do it. Here, sit on that trunk.'

Martin took a handful of her thick, rich hair. He knew the only problem he had was to stop his hands from shaking.

'How do you want it, madam?' It would be easier, he thought, to be in character.

'Just short. Be brave.'

The scissors were small, so it wasn't possible to cut the hair without lifting up lengths of it between thumb and forefinger.

Lift. Cut. Lift. Cut.

He was aware how his forefinger traced the slight undulation in Louise's scalp above her ears, the soft give of the ears when his fingers brushed against them. He cut where her hair grew from its crown and marvelled at the spring of it, the strength of it. He angled her head slightly and she responded to the slightest pressure. As the hair fell around her, neither spoke. Miguel, from across the clearing, watched.

Perhaps, Martin thought, he'd have his own story to tell once this was all over. He imagined the groups standing around him, on the fallen blossom, as he told them about his girlfriend.

'Yeah,' he'd go, 'half French, half American.'

'Cool.'

Martin tipped Louise's head down and lifted up the first hank of hair from the back of her neck. He cut it. He ran his hands through the hair that still fell over her shoulders and lifted another hank. He uncovered a mole the size of a pinhead. He cut till it was all gone. Down the back of her neck, briefly still lowered, trailed a line of golden hairs, so light only such a moment could show them.

'All done?' she asked.

'Almost,' he said and circled her, evening up the roughest of his cuts.

Louise had sensed his concentration throughout. The silence was part of it, but so too was the way his fingers had lingered – oh, the tiniest length of time – on her scalp or on her shoulder; and how, when he had first gathered up her hair to reveal her neck, she'd noticed a discernible intake of breath. She had sensed him behind her at the swimming hole too; sensed the excitement he'd felt as their thighs touched when the photograph was being taken. She felt from him something she could accept or deflect, something constant that, in this place at least, she could trust.

'*Qué linda!*' It was Eduardo, behind them. For the first time Louise felt exposed and ran her hands over the thick pelt of her hair.

'What? Have you been spying on us?' said Martin.

'On what? On you and me?' said Louise lightly, and the intimacy Martin had felt evaporated in the warm air.

Martin felt exposed again when Melanie exploded at Louise, then turned on him for the 'mess' he'd made of her 'baby's beautiful hair'.

'Did you never think of consulting me about whether it was a good idea?'

'Never,' said Louise, and she stood in the clearing, with her cropped hair and her shoulders pulled back. Like a warrior princess, thought Martin. A warrior princess who had commanded him to act and he had willingly obeyed.

'Am I the sole parent in all this?' Melanie spat at Jacques as she turned from them all.

Every time he saw Louise over the next couple of days he felt the web of intimacy grow again, threatening to ensnare him, so that he had to fight his way out of it – though if he could remember the exact tone in which she'd said 'You and me?' as if the idea were ridiculous, the threads broke at once. Because his powerlessness felt to him like shame, he avoided both Louise and Eduardo as far as was possible in the confines of the camp. It was the card game that brought Martin back to Louise and then brought the three of them together.

It had begun as the closest any of them had had to fun for many days. An even playing field at last. Only Rafael could have sanctioned it. But Louise had watched with a gathering horror as her father became a stranger to her. The pride she'd thought he carried for them all was revealed as mere aggression that until this moment had lacked the opportunity to express itself. The competition of the card game had stripped from Jacques an awareness of where they were and quite who they were dealing with. When he began pushing Miguel, Martin knew there could only be one possible outcome. Yet it had shocked Louise to see her strong father so humbled, retching on the ground like a sick dog.

Melanie had wanted more from her and called her disloyal; but her own displays of loyalty didn't appear to make Jacques feel any more warmly towards her. His shame was so deep, an arm of comfort was like salt in his wounds. He stayed in his shelter, nursed his pain, passed blood, and sulked.

Violence had entered the encampment. It was a time to lie low, to expiate. Martin's parents huddled over their notebooks. He and Louise drifted as far as they dared to the corner of the clearing, where Eduardo stood sole guard.

'Asshole. My father's an asshole.' Louise bared her teeth as she said it.

Martin shrugged. He wanted to tell her that there was something brave if foolhardy about her father's challenge, but he couldn't find the will to contradict her.

'And when he called Miguel a "big ape" – I couldn't believe my ears. Call him a thug, murderer – anything – but an *ape*. Jesus, that man's my father.'

'He's not so bad.' Eduardo's soft voice came with an undertow of sadness. 'You should not be so hard on him.'

'And why not?' said Louise.

'It's like you said: he's your father.'

'Yeah. And who are you anyway?' Louise's question came with force, as if she had been saving it up for the first good opportunity to ask it. Martin looked at

Eduardo and saw how his eyes met Louise's and did not flinch. Eduardo smiled slightly, lifted his head back and, as his body twisted, sang:

> *'I'm a Chicago mobster,*
> *I'm a fairy queen,*
> *I'm each godforsaken place*
> *My guitar's ever been . . .'*

'*Test Drive?*' gasped Louise. 'You like Test Drive?'

'*Hombre,* I *love* Test Drive.'

'Martin?'

He shook his head. 'I . . . em . . .'

'You really got to get into Test Drive,' Louise said. 'They're pure energy.'

'Sure, I'll just nip down to the store now and pick up their latest.'

'Good one, Marty,' said Louise.

She laughed, but Martin felt a small bitterness at how his failing had excluded him. He turned to Eduardo: 'Like Louise said, Eduardo, *who are you*?'

'I am Eduardo. I am a guerrilla.'

'We know the first,' said Louise, 'but you'll have to explain the second.'

'OK,' said Eduardo, 'I will tell you why . . .'

* * *

Both Eduardo's parents had worked at the university. They'd known Rafael's father there, but he was a number of years older and held a more senior position. Besides, his parents hadn't stayed long at the island university. They wanted to travel and both secured posts at a university in Chicago. There was a growing interest in the literature of the Conquest, and that was where his father had specialized. His mother, on the other hand, was more concerned with the developing literature of the island, particularly in emerging poets, like the young and talented Rafael Portuondo. Portuondo had only published a thin pamphlet, but with its mixture of sensual and political imagery it had created quite a stir. *Island Lover*, Eduardo remembered, had been his own mother's favourite poem and so had become one of his also.

> 'No one can impose a curfew on your beauty.
> No one can send a police patrol around my heart.
> And if they drive our love underground
> Like a secret river
> It will still be cool and sweet . . .'

Eduardo had attended the early years of high school in Chicago. He missed his grandmother and the close-knit intimacy of the island, but he marvelled at snow and at the easy availability of the latest PlayStation and the latest Test Drive CD. Test Drive had been formed in Chicago – its members had come from the housing precincts Eduardo had been told to avoid. 'There are many ways to find freedom,' his father used to say. Test Drive had certainly found one. Their music was the sound of walls breaking down. Eduardo and a couple of friends began to jam in the basement of his house – Test Drive numbers mostly, with a couple of their own raw compositions – and were aiming for a high-school gig when his parents announced they were returning to the island.

'It's time to go back,' his father said simply. 'There's a possibility for change, and your mother and I, and some time you, Eduardo, can play a part in the transformation of our island.'

Eduardo paused, respecting the memory of his father's words.

'And that is what happened. But their timing was bad. What they saw as opportunity was only a tiny seed of democracy. They returned just when the war got dirty.'

'The war?' said Louise.

'Yes, that is really what it became. A war carried out underground – its signs blood-stained basements and unmarked graves. A war fought by torturers and death squads. Within two months both of my parents had been "disappeared".'

'Disappeared?' said Martin.

'Yes. Eliminated. Got rid of. *Liquidated.*'

'But how?' said Louise.

'About that I try not to think. But one thing I can tell you is that this small, dirty war will not be a secret from the world for much longer.'

Martin and Louise nodded. It felt strange for them to share such thoughts with one of their captors. Louise glanced up at the forest canopy and felt giddy.

'So that is who I am,' said Eduardo. 'But I am also "a Chicago mobster". I am Tony Kurlansky, and here I am with my band, Test Drive, for a one-off performance in the heart of nowhere. Is my lead guitarist ready?'

'Ready and *on fire,*' said Louise.

'Is my drummer in position?'

'I don't really know any–'

'Oh, come on, Marty, Test Drive's drummer's

immense. Just get into it. Use your thighs or something.'

'A thigh-drum?'

'That's the one!'

'OK, Test Drivers,' said Eduardo. 'We're going on a burn-up! It's a one and a two and a three . . .

'Everywhere I go
I feel you breathin'
Down my neck –
Baby, you're turnin' me
Into a paranoid wreck . . .'

Eduardo peeled his T-shirt off and waved it over his head as he scissor-jumped and then spun around with one foot rooted to the spot. His singing and dancing caused a couple of parrots to rise from their perches – pure blue and green patches fluttering above their heads.

'But, baby, can't you
Feel my breath
Turned on you like fire –
These red-hot flames
Tell of my desire . . .'

Louise played air guitar as if her life depended on it. Martin lowered his head and drummed on his thighs, trying to lay down a beat behind words Eduardo would sometimes deliver like a punch and at others tease out till they broke into screams. He felt sweat pouring down the back of his neck and down the sides of his ribcage; but he drummed on till he was beating out a tune that was completely new. And somewhere, woven into this new rhythm, was the strangest thought: *Eduardo is OK.*

To Maria they looked like the flustered birds in the forest, flailing around as if their senses had left them. But there was no space for ruffled feathers here: what could Eduardo be thinking of?

'*Ya está bien! Están locos? Qué están haciendo?*'

'*Disculpa,*' said Eduardo. 'They are not *locos* – crazy – just letting off a little steam.'

'And you? What do you do, Eduardo? Leaving your weapon lying there on the grass. Like you're a child.'

Eduardo shrugged. He'd picked up his T-shirt and, breathing heavily, was wiping it over his face and his smooth chest.

'*Cuidado!*' Maria said. 'Remember who we all are

here, yes?' Then to Martin and Louise: 'To your shelters. Now.'

'Jesus,' said Louise. 'I'm getting so pissed with all of this!'

The next day they drifted to the same place. But it was a quieter, more composed Eduardo who stood guard now – back to the reserved interpreter of the first days. Louise trailed her frustration from the previous day.

'And our parents! *God, our parents.* My father just sits in the shelter like a kid, nursing his shame. My mother can't find the right words, as usual . . .'

'And mine seem barely here.'

'Exactly. So, Eduardo' – she stood up now and approached him – 'what is supposed to stop me walking right out of here?'

'You would starve to death.'

'I don't care.'

'Miguel would track you.'

'Miguel does not scare me.'

'He should.'

'Well, he doesn't any more. None of you scare me any more, so what's to stop me walking?'

With each question, Louise had moved closer to

Eduardo. She was almost as tall as he was and she stood before him now, her shoulders back, her head raised and a slightly taunting smile on her lips. What would you dare? she seemed to be saying.

Every nerve in Eduardo's body and in his face was still. Before Louise, he was impassive, rooted as one of the palm trees that surrounded them.

Martin saw all the energy with which Louise had confronted Eduardo break upon him until, drained, her shoulders slumped and she stepped back from him.

'Why would you not let me go?' she asked.

'Because I could not let you go.'

'But just then, what would you have done to stop me?'

'Please. Do not insult my parents' memory. I do not even know what suffering they had to bear. How can I forget that? Believe me, I would have stopped you.'

'And if they have to kill us, what then?'

'I've been living each day as it comes since my parents disappeared. This is today.'

Later Martin wondered if that had been the moment Louise finally fell in love with Eduardo – the moment when the bars may as well have fallen from the cage, for she stayed willingly now where he held her, taking each day as a gift.

'Come on then, Marty, if we're going to stay around here, there have to be changes. I can't bear another night with my parents – and I bet you feel the same.'

CHAPTER SIX

you think we don't listen

The room in the police station was bare apart from the scarred wooden table and a chair. Mason was wearing a shirt splashed with red and green parrots, and shorts and sandals. He looked up at Gabriel and shook his head sympathetically. The days in solitary had left Gabriel unshaven and weak. Under the single light bulb his skin appeared pallid and grey. Cousin Pablo was leaning against the wall with the same bored impatience he'd shown at Gabriel's home.

'*Mi amigo,*' Mason began, the vowels slithering into each other in the heat of the windowless room.

'Why am I here?' said Gabriel. 'I do jobs for Island Adventure. That's all.'

'*Espérate!* Not so fast,' said Mason. 'Don't you want to hear what I've been doing? Sure you do. This is such a pretty island. The windsurfing, the snorkelling is out of this world. You've got to take these opportunities while you can, and Pablo here has been a most obliging guide.'

Pablo looked over and nodded in acknowledgement.

'I do not play games,' said Gabriel.

'No games. Quite right. Let's get straight to the heart of the matter. There's no one around here who has the knowledge of these parts that you do. We've learned from those who've known you since you were small that your father led you everywhere around here, that he taught you–'

'Yes,' said Gabriel, 'he taught me these lands are sacred.'

'That may be as you see it,' said Mason, 'but there are other forces at work here, you see. And, boy, you're dealing with something way over your head.'

'It's our country, our land and you've no right–' Gabriel's rising voice was silenced when Pablo swung his truncheon into his stomach. He fell to his knees, retching.

'Hey, Pablo,' said Mason, 'there's no need for that. No need for that at all.'

Pablo held up his palms and shrugged.

'Look,' Mason continued, 'we know your sympathies, your situation, your knowledge. We know you're in this. But hey, that's not what's most important. What's important is where we go from here. Now come on, Pablo, help Gabriel up.'

Gabriel brushed off Pablo's hand and got shakily to his feet, his arms around his stomach.

'Thing is,' said Mason, 'you don't help, we will be forced to act.'

'So act,' spat Gabriel.

'Now hold on there a minute. Let's get straight exactly what's at stake here. Nickel is one of the most important metals for the developed world. Combined with other metals – iron, copper, chromium and zinc – it makes alloys that are used for all kinds of things. But to make it simple, most nickel is used to make stainless steel. Have you any idea the amount of stainless steel a country the size of America needs? Probably not, but let me tell you, for the military alone the demands are huge – more than you can possibly imagine.'

Pablo knew, though, or he could easily imagine. He saw the skyscrapers of *Nueva York* shining stainlessly in the sun.

'And do you know how many nickel mines there are in the whole of the USA to meet that need? One. One lonely mine. So don't think for a minute that

America can ignore what's happening in places that keep it . . .'

'. . . a shining beacon for the world,' said Pablo, looking very pleased with himself.

'Something like that,' said Mason. 'So let me spell out the options to you. Number one, we can wait. Not too long, but long enough. You see, your boys are very clever, so we need to be clever too. They hold a bunch of tourists and it looks like they have power. But, you see, we hold you. You don't help and we hold you indefinitely. I can think of any number of charges we could bring against you. Number two, any rights you do have are only courtesy of United Nickel. It's only our involvement in this, our desire to bring it to a satisfactory conclusion, that's stopping you from being put directly in the care of the authorities here. You know that would not be so pleasant.'

Pablo nodded agreement.

'Number three. Think of your family without your wages. You know what? Your sweet mother – Pilar, yes? – comes here every day asking for you. She looks worn down with it all. Think of your dying father.'

A nerve flitted up the side of Gabriel's face.

'You think we don't understand. You think we don't

listen. How, you ask, can a huge multinational like United Nickel understand what's happening on a tiny island? Of course we understand. Times change and it's hard. The world's full of envy and that's hard too. But these things fade, the world settles again into its new groove. But, *amigo,* there are always winners and losers. And that's your choice, Gabriel. It's a man's choice, and you're making it for yourself and for your family. What I can offer you is your freedom and an increased pension for your father to ease the pain of his last days. I mean, there are drugs. No reason why the poor man has to suffer so.'

'What do you want of me?'

'That's the question I've been wanting us to get to since we met, Gabriel, and I'm very pleased you've finally decided to ask it. That's the mark of a wise man.'

Oh, look on and learn, thought Mason. This is how to carry out a successful interrogation. It requires experience and sophistication – psychology, for Christ's sake – not simply hanging a guy from a meat-hook and beating his kidneys till he passes out.

Gabriel was grinding his teeth so hard, he couldn't understand why they didn't crumble to dust in his mouth. Yet still a traitor tear escaped and made its way slowly down his cheek.

'Trust me, a man's decision it is. Like I said, Gabriel, your friends – the guerrillas, the freedom fighters, whatever you want to call them – they're my old friends too. We meet them all over the world. They don't like change, don't like the way of the world. They think what they're doing is for good. Oh, I know they're not evil men – hell, they may even be heroes. But they just can't see the way forward. Sure they'll have to have their knuckles rapped, do some time, but I don't think they deserve to die like animals hunted down in the forest. I fear for them though. For if we have to go in and get them, that's what will happen. People will die.'

More than anything, Gabriel could hear his father's screams of pain in the night.

'Sure as hell, people will die. Unless someone can lead them all down to safety, to a place where the whole sorry episode can be concluded with as little damage as possible. So the world can start turning again. There are many ways to be a hero, Gabriel, and I mean, really, what's the alternative?'

CHAPTER SEVEN

promise me something

There had been less opposition to the building of another shelter than either of them could have imagined. Martin thought it was all down to Louise. She seemed to glow with defiance as she told Rafael what she and Martin were going to do and demanded each be given a machete for the task.

Louise put all she had into cutting and weaving the frame of the hut. And, though Martin helped and at times lost himself in the task, he couldn't stop himself every so often just watching her body, shining with sweat, become a perfect arc, before the machete cleaved through another branch.

'Come on, Marty, homemaker,' she called to him. 'We need at least three more of these.'

Their parents understood what they were doing without asking. For the past couple of years at home, had they not been insisting on more isolated, private rooms? *Keep out. Unless you're an alien.* So they let them go now as they were always going to one day. They needed space. They weren't children any more. You can't hold them to you for ever. And for their part, they were tired: tired of being judged, tired of exposing frailty and shame. Especially here, surrounded by guns, in a forest clearing where there was nowhere to hide. Let them get on with it, see how they fare. Sure, it's earlier than they might have wished, but which one of us has the energy to take them on?

Tony, Carol and Melanie looked to Jacques one last time. But he turned from them and shrugged as if it had nothing to do with him. As if somehow the dark bruises he wore across his stomach were *their* fault. From now on, each man for himself.

The shelter they had built was inexpert. The thatch had not been closely woven enough, so the edge was taken off the sheer darkness where they lay.

'Well, this is an improvement,' said Louise. 'Marty?'

'Yes,' said Martin. His chest was tight and his voice when it came was thin and ragged.

'God, your father and his poetry.'

'I know.'

'What do you miss most, Marty?'

'A burger and a cold Coke come to mind.'

'Yeah, junk food. Heaps of it. Bring it on.'

'With ketchup.'

'*Unlimited* . . . What else do you miss?'

'I . . . I don't know.'

'Well, what's the first thing you'll do when this is all over?'

'Check out Test Drive, I suppose.'

'Yeah, you do that. You'll love them.'

'You?'

'I think I'll get myself a tattoo.'

'Like a little bluebird on your arm or something?'

'No. More like a huge set of wings across my back like Tony Kurlansky has.'

'Wild. Angel wings?'

'Could be. Oh, I don't know. It's like, you know, Marty, life's just more . . . more . . .'

'More what?'

'Jesus, I really don't know how to say it – just more *everything* than I thought it was.'

'So?'

'So, I guess I want more than I thought I did, that's all.'

'Like a bigger tattoo.'

'Yeah. You got it. A *beast* of a tattoo.'

They lay in silence, staring at the black thatch. Martin felt he might catch fire no matter what – whether he continued to lie in his own space or whether he stretched out and touched Louise. But he knew he must not touch her. That would only lead to a shame he could not bear. Though there was a chance that perhaps, in some corner of her heart, Louise might know what he was feeling and how painful the restraint was and recognize in it the love he had to give. He hoped this might be so as he lay and waited for her to make her move.

A bird he had not heard before sang softly in the night.

'Marty?'

'Yes.'

'You still awake?'

'Yes, I'm still awake.'

'I'm going out of the shelter. I don't know for how long.'

'Eduardo?'

'Like I say, I don't know for how long. Marty, you know, I could've ended up with all kinds of complete assholes on this trip. It's one of the luckiest things in my life that I ended up with you. I want you to know that I just feel we're always going to be friends. But I need you to promise me something.'

'What?'

'That no matter what happens from now on, this remains a secret between us.'

'You and Eduardo?'

'Promise me, Marty?'

How could it be that her eyes shone so in the darkness as she knelt over him in the shelter?

'OK, I promise.'

'No, Marty – the promise, it's got to sound *more.*'

'More what?'

'More like you really mean it. I want this to be our secret – a secret that only I can break. Take my hands and promise.'

'I, Martin Phillips . . . *promise.*' It was true: one touch of her and he was burning.

'Now go,' he said. 'Please.'

Louise dipped down and kissed his cheek, then turned and crawled out of the shelter. She walked quickly to the edge of the encampment where Eduardo was waiting.

Miguel watched her from the shadows. He shrugged. Eduardo, young Eduardo, let him live while he is young, while he can. Let a young woman run her hands over his smooth back. El Taino's hands, he thought sadly, were probably the last hands he would feel on the welts of his own back.

She loved the way his top lip came to a small point in its middle like a tiny beak, and that when he smiled it disappeared completely. She loved how his teeth were so straight that if a ruler were placed against them there would be no gaps. She loved the way he grew so serious, so suddenly that his eyes became, as some poet she'd read in high school had described them, 'windows to his soul'. She loved the life she sensed in him – its darkness and its loss and its blinding Test Driving light. His fingers were long, and he used his hands like punctuation marks whenever he spoke. He ran them back over his loosely curled hair. And, when he thought she wasn't watching, used them to scratch between his legs.

And what could he love about her? she wondered, aware of how little they wore and of how few were the secrets they could keep, living day by day so close together. But she could not bear to think of her own question.

'I love your boy's hair,' he said.

'Thank you very much.'

'It is, as the French say, *gamin.*'

'And what does that mean?'

'Oh, I don't know. Youthful or something like that. It's one of the untranslatables.'

'And that's all you like?'

'No, that's only the beginning. But it is hard to find these untranslatable words.'

She nodded, feeling both of them were now speaking in a foreign language – and for a moment she stood on the edge of something, as she had paused at the edge of the pool – it seemed so long ago now – scared of what unfamiliar creatures might inhabit the water.

'Then don't use words,' she said finally and lifted her face to his. And so he told her how he loved her eyes, just as they were closing, and how he loved her skin, in parts still so white that anything could be written on it – anger, frustration, desire. And he loved the arms that came around him and the hands that entwined themselves in his hair, determined to hold onto this world she had discovered for each and every day she could. And he loved the hunger in her that was as fresh as his was for her and yet that already knew what would satisfy it.

'Now you know,' he whispered breathlessly.

'Yes, oh yes, I'm getting the messages loud and clear.'

Across the clearing she caught sight of Miguel's silhouette, his hand raised in greeting. Eduardo waved back. Louise, flustered, began to rise from his chest.

'Here,' he said, 'it's all right. Miguel is all right with us.'

Louise eased herself back down beside him.

'Eduardo?'

'Yes.'

'You said once you'd tell me the story of what happened to Miguel's back.'

'Ay, *preciosa,* it's a long story. And it's hard to tell Miguel's story without telling El Taino's too, for that's where the story begins.'

'Well, I'm going nowhere and I'd like to know.'

CHAPTER EIGHT

not anyone's slave

Before he became El Taino, he was known simply as José or José the Thief. He used to say, 'It's the tourists that make me do it. They are *locos, simplemente locos. Locos* maybe, but they had what José wanted more than anything: *dólares.* With *dólares* José could buy leather boots, and sometime he could buy a heavy gold chain for his neck, like a baseball star, and a couple of gold rings too. With *dólares* José could make himself a man to be reckoned with.

He had begun as a confidence trickster, pitting his wits against the tourists.

'Hello, my friend,' he'd begin, almost walking backwards as he spoke, so there was no avoiding him. 'You new in town? You *Americano,* yes? *Inglés? Frances? Deutsch?* You see, we welcome the world.'

Louise remembered such characters in the first days they'd spent in the capital. Her father had tried to brush them off, but her mother and she had responded at first to the feigned warmth of the greeting, the humour there seemed to be in it: you know I'm faking it and I know you know, but hey, I *do* know places to go, and you are a little bit lost in the narrow streets that can turn so quickly into darkness, into shadows in doorways. She found it easy to picture El Taino turning to the tourists and smiling a fake smile.

'What you want? You know the bars? I take you to the famous bars. I know them all – where all the most famous *mafioso* dons drank. You want to see? To hear the story of when Don Rosselli was killed. There is still blood on the restaurant walls. This is a crazy country, you are thinking, where they leave the blood of dead men on the walls.'

A story, the tourists would think. Well, why not? They'd sit in some small dingy bar with a faded newsprint photograph framed on the wall, somewhere a splash of red paint. Someone would sing for them – one of those island songs that spoke of endless longing – and they'd be served cocktails at inflated prices. The minute the notes were handed over – *dólares*, only *dólares* – a chill entered the conversation. The energy seemed to go from their guide and the naïve tourists wondered whether any place could match one's imagining of it. Louise's father was irritated to find himself among their number.

'Come on, Jacques,' she remembered her mother saying. 'It's hardly worth getting upset over – a few dollars.'

'I just *hate* getting ripped off. I told you he wasn't right. You've got to listen to me, Melanie.' And he walked on ahead of them both into a well-lit plaza.

José's cuts from these affairs afforded him his first gold ring – not as heavy as he would have liked, but enough to catch the light. And he was able to buy good food for his family – sausages, fish and cheese. Still it did not placate his father.

'It's not a job,' his father raged at him. 'You bring me shame.'

'No,' José said, 'I bring food for our table. I bring more than rice and beans.'

'Oh yes, oh yes, you do. And do you know the flavour that is missing from all this food you bring? The taste of pride is nowhere in it.'

'You wait!' José had shouted at him. 'You wait and see.'

He saw the city teeming with possibilities for him, with more money than he could ever earn as an unofficial tourist guide.

Again it was the tourists' own fault really. *Locos. Simplemente locos.* They left wallets on bar tops. They wore trousers and waistcoats and money-belts that said, *Money's in here. You'll need to be quick, you'll need a certain sleight of hand, but we'll be careless or flustered and our anxiety will help you.*

Louise remembered the city, its sense of danger, and her mother's endless zips and secret pockets. As she had stood in her T-shirt and shorts, swaying to the music that was everywhere, she had felt a sense of irresponsibility distance her from her mother.

Of course, what allowed it all to happen was not the Saint of Pilfering. There was no special agent like that looking out for José. What was letting it happen for as long as it did was luck. Lady Luck, if you like – José did like the ladies – and a certain local admiration for a rogue, someone with balls enough to fleece these dim tourists with their loud voices and their fat wallets.

José's love affair with Lady Luck finished when the police force was told that such behaviour was putting off tourists coming to the island. They were taking their precious *dólares* elsewhere. A clean-up was what was required.

* * *

The short truncheon that broke two of José's fingers on his right hand was protecting a wallet lying on the scarred counter top of the popular harbourside bar of El Marisco. As José bent to cradle his hand, the man in T-shirt and shorts, who had whipped the truncheon from a beach bag, declared himself to the astonished tourists as their protector. He then apologized for the disturbance caused and presented the wide-eyed husband with the wallet, as if it were a medal on a velvet cushion.

'Why – uh, thank you,' said the man.

'And him?' said his wife, pointing to the thief, one of whose wrists was already padlocked to the bar.

'*Señora*, please not to trouble yourself. Let us to take care of him. And enjoy your stay in Santa Clara. You will find all the rest of us, I hope and pray, to be honest.'

'It was the gold flashing that gave him away,' the policeman announced at the reception area to the prison, 'so he's better off without it, don't you think?' There were whoops of agreement. He wrenched the ring from one of José's broken fingers – his finger a living flame that made him gasp. He threw the ring in the air, caught it and pocketed it with a smile. If only that had been the end of it. But no, blows had rained down on him from all the policemen there – 'Flash little shit'; 'Only one crappy ring' – so that when he woke up the next day in the cold stone cell, it wasn't only his fingers that throbbed. So too did his ribs, and one of his eyes had almost closed, gummed with blood.

His swollen hand looked naked to him. He was the nothing they said he was. He was the nothing his father always said he was destined to be. When he had been hauled through the streets, those who had once looked at him with admiration now looked on him with pity or shame. He was the nothing they'd always seen behind the shiny surface.

What was time to a nothing? He had no idea how many days he'd spent in the cell, eating the slop they threw in to him, binding his broken fingers as well as he could with strips of T-shirt he'd torn off with his teeth. At night he lay on the fouled mattress with his hand across his chest and felt his fingers throbbing. They would knit in their own way but he knew light-fingered José the Thief was no more.

On one of these nights his cell door opened. A figure filled the light and then was thrown into the cell with the same care that a side of beef might be thrown onto a truck. José could only make out the black shape of him in the darkness.

The new prisoner moaned. It was the eeriest sound – a creature-in-suffering sound – and José thought perhaps the only way to quell it was to approach the creature, to see what might be done for it.

'My . . . *back*.' The words erupted from him as if they'd been pushed up from the depths of his chest. José put an arm round him tentatively, but quickly withdrew it. As it came into contact with his wet, clammy back, the man had made a high-pitched animal sound. José too was now in shock, not simply at the sticky wetness but at the fact that his fingers had momentarily felt the runnels in the flesh that held the blood.

'*Jesus*.' José sighed. What had this man done? And what was to be done for him now in the cold dirt of the cell, lying on his front, his head twisted, his mouth gasping for air?

José reached out his hand again and stroked the man's brow and ran his palm back from the broad forehead, over the tightly curled hair. Then, in the darkness, he could make out the white of an eye turned to him. '*Gracias, hermano*,' came gargling from the man's throat.

Early the next morning a bucket of salt water was brought to their cell.

'Put it on his back before the scabs form or it could be over for your new friend,' said the guard.

'But he needs–' José began.

'Look, this is the best I can do. Don't ask for more or there'll be three of us in there.'

By the thin daylight that filtered into the cell from a window too high to give them its view of the rocks and the sea, José examined the six deep welts in the man's back for any foreign bodies that might threaten infection. Then he paused – memories of how as a child he'd grazed his knee on a rock and how the sea had stung.

'*Por favor*,' the man said. Then, '*Mi nombre es* Miguel.'

'José.'

'José.' Miguel nodded.

'I'm sorry,' said José.

'*De nada*.'

Miguel gripped the sides of the mattress and José poured the salt water into the sluiceways of his back. Two forces were at work in Miguel then. In one he fought to turn away from the water, to rise up from the mattress, to escape from José, to curse him with all his might. In the other, he fought as if the mattress were a demon that must for his survival be pinioned to the cell floor. His shoulders rippled with the ferocity of his struggle; in his arms veins like ropes pumped the necessary blood and only occasionally did he emit that animal sound José had first heard from him. It was a fight of great intensity, but short-lived. Miguel's breathing evened and his eyes closed in exhaustion.

In these first days there was little conversation between the two, for this was a place they'd come to that somehow obliterated all others. Of course they'd known of its existence – the regime made no secret of where its deviants would end up, be they political, sexual or criminal. Their pasts would be washed from them here. They would be numbers, units of suffering: time would abandon them at the gate. José and Miguel became familiar with neighbouring screams of pain, but also with screams of anger and despair. They tried as best they could to pay them no attention. At first they paid little attention to each other either, except as physical presences, in the way that animals at opposite ends of a field will sense the company of one another and gain some blind comfort from that.

Soon the wounded man began to heal: the blood congealed and huge scabs formed, beneath which the skin began to stretch over the trenches the flails had made.

'What did you do to deserve such a torture?' José asked one day.

'Union,' said Miguel.

'Union?'

'Workers' rights.'

There was silence. José had heard of those who campaigned for workers' rights. He had even skirted one of their demonstrations on his way to the tourist marina. Passionate men and women with megaphones speaking of their burden, their obligations to their families, to the future generations 'who will live on our beautiful island'. But he had also heard how the government opposed the movement, portraying its leaders as leeches, stirrers, puppets of foreign governments.

'And what do they want?' Quitano had asked once more. 'What would give them the greatest pleasure? I tell you – to see our island divided, our progress stalled. On behalf of our people, I, we, this government, will not tolerate it!'

'Why you?' José asked.

'I led a strike the day after the ordinance banning demonstrations against the state.'

'You are a brave man – or a foolish one.'

'I am not anyone's slave,' Miguel flashed back with the first anger in his voice. 'No, not a slave, though my blood comes from those who came to this island in chains.'

'I didn't mean–'

'It's all right, *amigo*. Do not think I am a particularly brave man. I am rather one who tests the waters, who wants bread for the workers, decent pay for families to live on, an end to corruption.'

'And look where it's got you.'

'I tell you, it's got me thinking. Quitano has shown his hand. I know now the way is not through workers' shows of strength. They will be mercilessly crushed.'

'There is another way?'

'There is. But it is not so direct.'

'What is it?'

'*Basta ya, compañero*. All these questions for me. What are you in this shit-hole for? Come on, don't be shy. Are you a *maricón*? Do you dress up in women's clothing? Did you piss on a statue of General Quitano?'

He had called him *compañero* – 'comrade' – perhaps in jest. He had certainly joked about his possible offences.

'*Soy ladrón.* I am a thief.' José did not mutter the words. Each syllable rang out clearly in the fetid air of the cell. '*Soy ladrón.*' The final syllable of the Spanish fell heavily, like something laid down that was naked, inescapable.

'*Sí, señor,* one of your punishments is to share a cell with a common thief. I steal from tourists.'

Miguel nodded slowly, giving José's admission proper attention.

'Perhaps, comrade, what you say is true. But you are not *only* a thief.'

'How can you know that, when all you know of me is living in this place?'

'I know. I know *from* living with you in this place. Comrade, you are so much more than a thief.'

José felt his eyes burn with the tears that rolled down his cheeks in the darkness. Miguel's rough hands fell on his shoulders and circled them a couple of times. Truly, Miguel wondered, which of us here is really the wounded one?

'When we get out of here, come with me,' he said. 'There is someone I'd like you to meet.'

'But how can we ever . . . ?'

'A time will come, believe me.'

'What person should I meet?'

'The less you know, the better. All I will say is that there are people working in different ways. My torturers could not know it, but when I asked myself, What must I do now? they wrote the answer on my back.'

When the door was opened and they were brought out the first time, the sea air hit them with such power it was like a wind that poured through a building made of sand. They held onto each other and gulped in the air.

For Pepe, the transvestite, with his black haunted eyes and his bruised body, the promise of freedom was too much. He broke away from the rest of the group and jumped the castle wall. Perhaps he'd thought the waves, far below, would break his fall and that he'd swim the white-flecked waters of the bay to become himself again. But the water withdrew from the rock and his leap was too weak. 'Like a girl's,' one of the guards said later. His broken body lay on the rocks. The splayed limbs made it look as if he were still running.

Miguel took José's forearm and pulled him firmly back into the body of the work party.

Each day thereafter, as they were led outside and taken to the Convent of Santa Catarina, which they were renovating as part of the Colonial Tourist Trail, they felt their strength returning. Working in Miguel's shadow, José began to feel the stirrings of another life forming in the nothing he'd thought he was. He watched Miguel apply himself to the building work they were given to do and, protecting his damaged hand as best he could, he shirked nothing. He stood beside Miguel in the cool of the cloister as Miguel told the foreman that there was a better way to restore the old convent, reminding him that this was not just work for today, but for History. 'Even you, foreman, will be judged some day.'

'Is that a fact?' the foreman said. 'Well, have a good sniff. Can you smell it – the dust of all that withered passion? That's the closest you're going to get to a woman for the next thirty years. So save your judgements for yourself, asshole.'

By the third day they had a plan.

The convent had a false wall. Miguel would break through it, then drag a huge mahogany dresser over the gap. At the end of the day they would both go through the break in the wall and Miguel would, with his fingertips, pull the dresser over the gap behind them. It was audacious and difficult, but it worked.

They found the passage led to a small window at the back of the convent. From there they had to jump down to the ground. José landed badly on his ankle. Miguel picked him up in the darkness and ran with him through ill-lit streets, his eyes the eyes of a desperate man keeping everyone at a distance. They reached a small wooden hut by the railway. There, Miguel lowered José onto an iron bed and turned silently to the owner, an old man so bent over he had to twist his head to look up at Miguel. His eyes glistened in the lamplight. The last things José saw before sleep consumed him were a black and white photograph of a slight but wiry young black boxer, peering at him arrogantly behind raised gloves, and the grotesquely swollen knuckles of the old man, his ruined fists like paws on Miguel's shoulders.

He woke next morning with the jolt of another prisoner's screams. But it was only the early morning train, hauling its way along a track that would lead it, haltingly, across the spine of the island to the opposite coast.

In the following days José learned that, in his

heyday, Pedro Juan Crespo – 'The Kid' – had owned over two hundred suits. He'd ridden in the back of open Cadillacs. And the girls! Every time a car he was in stopped, '*Chicas! Chicas! Chicas!*' But his American managers had found it more profitable to deny him the title fights he craved; to keep him always as 'The Contender'. So he'd fought on, till his fists seized shut and the pain became unbearable. He discovered far too late that they'd picked him clean as a bone.

Still, he hadn't lost hope. What they couldn't take from him was his experience, and he'd had some small success in training young boxers. One prospect in particular had looked bright – a young black heavyweight who'd brought a fierce intensity to each fight, but who was disdainful of the crowd's approval. He was the kind of fighter many people would turn up to see take a beating – box-office gold.

'But Miguel,' Pedro said, 'he would not fight in the expensive hotels. He would not do as he was told. So stubborn! Very soon no one would touch him.'

'I saw what happened to you, old man.'

'But maybe it could have been different.'

'Ah, maybe. But not with me.'

'Pity,' Pedro said, turning to José. 'What a left hook he had. And what a temper!'

'Well, I still have that, old man. So watch out!'

'Eh, José,' Pedro said, 'you fast?' He flung a fist at José's head. José ducked and felt the knuckles graze his ear.

'Not bad,' Pedro said, his grin showing off the three crooked teeth he had left.

'Quiet, old man,' Miguel said. 'Keep your old dreams to yourself.'

Pedro's daughter, Cristina, brought them fresh clothes and every day something to eat. She was slight like her father and José could see the handsome features of the young boxer in her tired face. But she hated to hear his stories.

'What has boxing done for him?' she asked no one in particular. 'But what else has he got left?'

A week later, wearing the clean clothes Cristina had brought and with the swelling in his ankle almost gone, José was led to a safe house in the old part of the city. There, Miguel introduced him to Rafael and Maria. The unions and the university radicals had shared platforms in the past, but Rafael's path had rarely crossed Miguel's, so he had a natural suspicion of José.

'What were you in *El Castillo* for?'

José hesitated. This was not the same place as the cell. He was confounded to find that his new-won strength had left him, that there was no honour or honesty in admitting his shame. With the eyes of the woman, Maria, fixed on him, Miguel took him back to the moment of his first confession.

'He was a thief. But he was never only a thief. And he is not the man he was when he went into *El Castillo*. None of us are. But I know what he is more than he does and I trust him with my life.'

Again José felt the sharpness behind his eyes; but he clenched his jaw and stemmed his tears. Rafael was looking at him and smiling.

'José, you, more than any of us here, resemble the first people of our island.'

José said nothing.

'With your bronze skin, your black hair, your almond eyes, you could be one of the Taino people.'

Miguel was smiling now – even the woman was – as Rafael continued: 'And you know they used to say the Taino people were wiped out early in the Conquest by war, disease and oppression. But it wasn't so. They went inland and became guerrilla fighters and continued to raise their children in the mountains and the forests and to maintain the original line.'

'El Taino,' said Miguel.

'Yes,' said Rafael, 'that's who you are. Come back to reclaim your country from the oppressor. El Taino.'

'Yes. Yes,' said José. 'From now on, José the Thief is no more – only El Taino.'

Eduardo was surprised at how moved he was himself in the telling of a story he had only heard. He turned to Louise, whose eyes were shining on him.

'So you see, *preciosa*,' he said, 'you see who these men are and you know now, I think, why I could never be the one to let you go free.'

CHAPTER NINE

nada por nada

The next day Martin watched the arrival of the small man from the tourist office, Gabriel, as intrigued as any of the others. Gabriel seemed slightly embarrassed by the greeting he received. He lowered his head and smiled sheepishly. Unusually for an islander, he turned from their embraces.

That night Martin talked with Louise about the significance of Gabriel's arrival; and about the revelation that Quitano, who sat at the heart of it all like a black spider, turned out to be Rafael's uncle.

For Martin such events were the only relief to the extreme tedium of the day. He lived only for the evening, to lie beside Louise, to feel her warmth against his own, though this closeness was almost unbearable. When finally she rose, after the night bird called, he found a silence enveloped him. It was not that he did not wish to speak, but that he could not. The words stuck in his throat, hooked there, and would not come out.

'Marty,' she said, 'don't take it badly.' He shook his head and shrugged in the darkness.

Louise never mentioned Gabriel or Quitano to Eduardo, never asked how many other secrets he was keeping from her. The day had been long for them too, and in whatever time they had, they wanted to talk about themselves.

'You know,' Eduardo said, 'you are your parents' daughter.'

'Don't say that.'

'I'm sorry.'

'I want to be *myself*.'

'You are, *preciosa*, you are.'

'But what do you mean? Tell me. I'm interested.'

'Like your parents, you have fight in you. You do not accept things as they are. I like that.'

'Maybe I will like that in myself too one day.'

'I hope so.'

'And you? Are you like your parents?'

'I like to think so. It was my dad who was Test Drive's number-one fan.'

'No!'

'Yes. And you know, sometimes I hated him for

that – for coming into my world. Such a small thing.'

'I'd like to have met them.'

Eduardo was silent. His brown eyes mournful.

'I know,' she said. 'It's nuts to talk like this.'

'No, it's just . . . it's maybe not the time to talk right now . . .'

The helicopter that passed overhead the next day was the sign for them all that this life would not go on for ever. Not that any of them thought it would, but there were times when, out of despair – or a secret joy – each of them had thought, Is there no end to this?

Louise began to think that they had been wrong, her mother and she, to separate time and geography, to imagine that either had any real meaning. 'How long are you away for this time?' her mother had asked. Or 'Where to this time?' sighing at the distance mentioned. But it was obvious now that space and time were one. She felt herself, in so few weeks, in a huge space, belying time. But that night even Louise was forced to acknowledge that the helicopter had signalled the beginning of the end.

Orders had been given for the break-up of the camp, so time was pressing. She held Eduardo's face in her hands and whispered to him the words that Julia, the old peasant woman, had all that time ago: '*Cuidado*, Eduardo, *cuidado*.'

Eduardo did not dismiss her words. He took the weight of her concern as he had the force of her challenge at the rim of the camp, but this time he nodded and smiled slightly at the pleasure of it. And Louise remembered, as well as the old woman's words, what Maria had said about the weightlessness of their lives – and she dismissed that with a smile of her own. For she felt, held in the balance of the life that was all around her – the fear and the desire and the restless green growth – her own life, not light with insignificance, *nada por nada*, as Maria had judged it, but holding its own, drawing on what surrounded her and becoming part of that too. And she kissed the face she held and thanked Eduardo, his hand cupped on her naked breast, for giving her the gift of herself.

Then it began to rain.

CHAPTER TEN

another life to live

When they came to the river, the morning sun had already dried them and the packs they carried. But the river was swollen from the rain that all night had drummed on the broad palms woven into their shelters. At first the river looked uncrossable, but Miguel gave the idea no thought. His feet were on the first two stepping stones and his hand held out before Rafael could pass judgement. But even Rafael was surprised that it was Martin who stretched out his hand and stepped onto the first stone. Martin gave Louise the briefest glance. She had made her choice, but he wanted to show her that he was still worthy – still one of them. A Test Driver. In Louise's words, 'Pure energy unplugged in the jungle.'

He could never get straight in his mind whether Miguel had been unable to reach his hand, when he had begun to twist and fall, or whether he had disdained it, knowing he would only endanger Martin. Or whether, worst of all, Martin had begun to withdraw his own hand in fear for his safety. Whichever of them made such a decision, Martin was forced to watch helplessly as Miguel twisted savagely, almost comically, before he finally fell. There was the sickening crack of his skull on the stone, then his blood bloomed in the water.

Martin allowed himself to be held, to hear his mother's draining sobs so close to him, he felt they would drown him. As soon as he was able, he withdrew into himself on the bank. He felt the blame of Maria and El Taino burning into his back.

'Nothing you could do,' said Louise. 'Nothing. None of us . . . about anything.'

She had lost the composure of the past few days. The space she and Eduardo had created was gone. From now on, it was made clear, they were to remain a tight group. They would camp close together and, in their closeness, she and Eduardo felt an ocean of distance open up between them.

It was then that the nostalgia began for a place they had so recently left – an encampment in the heart of a forest that was unreachable and vast. She had spent a lifetime there, she was sure of it: Eduardo and she.

If there were others there, they were no more important to them than were the trees and the birds.

Eduardo had told her the local belief that it was in the green heart of such a forest that God created man and woman with a song. '*The woman is born and the man is born,*' said the song. '*Together they will live and they will die. But they will be born again. They will be born and they will die again and be born again. They will never stop being born, because death is a lie.*' For those who believed, Eduardo had said, the song was not a promise, it was just the way things were.

Strange that she should find love, not at the high-school dances, not hanging about Starbucks, but in the middle of a forest. She closed her eyes and imagined Eduardo and herself still there. They were sitting round a fire. They were entwined as the sun rose, before striking camp and walking deeper and deeper into the dim green light where no one would find them.

But out of the forest, by the riverside, she found other forces at work. She had another life to live.

When El Taino pushed the muzzle of the machine gun into Jacques' neck for his stubborn refusal to stand at Miguel's graveside, she didn't see the 'asshole' she had seen during the card game. Instead there was a tired man, holding onto his dignity as he refused to acknowledge the man who'd humiliated him. He rose painfully slowly and turned to face them. His eyes briefly flared when they met Louise's as if to say, *This is for you. This is the man your father is.* It was the man who Eduardo had told her of.

She felt sharp pangs in her heart as she was forced to acknowledge that she was not and could never be free, walking the paths of the forest with Eduardo. The pain came to her in waves – exquisite and fresh – and she did not fight it.

She had never felt so alive, though all she shared with Eduardo now were scraps – a brush as they passed each other; a glance, like the one they shared at Miguel's burial. When Rafael spoke of the things that divided them all, Louise thought, I know, *I know*, and thanked Eduardo for what he had shared with her about El Taino and the dead Miguel.

CHAPTER ELEVEN
what scares you?

There was a small hut in the sandy soil and the thinned trees before they reached the beach. An old man with black weathered skin was sitting outside it, mending a fishing net. Rafael called to him. '*Hola, buenos días, señor.*'

'*Buenos días,*' said the old man. 'I think I know you. But what do you want of me?'

'We are in a struggle to make all our lives better – yours too. We will win, *compañero*, but in the meantime we are hungry.'

'*Amigos*, you will not go hungry here.'

The old man went into his hut and brought out a line with several fish hanging from it and an armful of plantain.

'This is all I have,' he said, 'apart from a little for myself. It was for the market tomorrow.'

'It is enough,' said Rafael. '*Gracias, abuelo*. You will be remembered.'

'*De nada,*' the old man said.

The hostages came onto the beach, blinking in the open light, like frightened creatures flushed from the forest. By the blue sea they looked at each other, at what time had done to them, with an understanding denied to them in the closed world of the forest.

Martin saw their ripped and soiled T-shirts, the ingrained red earth that was in their shorts. His mother was painfully thin. She'd bitten her nails down to the quick and her eyes looked one way, then another, as if they couldn't find rest. His father was shambling, distracted. His beard was matted and wild. Jacques, more lightly bearded, was a shrunken figure compared to his former self. He dragged his feet through the sand. A line of coin-sized sores, weeping pus, tracked down one of Melanie's shins. Down the centre of her hair, a band of grey marked the passage of time. And were their captors any better? El Taino too had bags under his eyes and trudged forward as if into an imaginary gale. Each of them had also lost weight, drained by a constant vigilance.

And then there was Louise. Crop-headed, her hair without the lustre it had once had, her body having almost retreated from the fullness it promised. Yet at the sight of the ocean her heart leaped. Her life inland in America had meant that she had never been able to quell that connection between the sea and vacation, and she felt the freedom surge through her that she always felt at the first glimpse of blue. And the freedom brought with it an optimism she realized had been missing from the depth of her love – always it had been shadowed. She had a thought: perhaps it will be possible to bring Eduardo into this freedom. It would be no stranger than what has already happened. Perhaps once this is all over and we're both far away. But even as she thought this, she knew nothing could be more precious to her than the times Eduardo and she had spent together, holding each other against the slight cool of the night, once talking had taken them as far as talking could. What she'd liked best was how they breathed together, breathed in the salty, earthy smell of them both – she felt she'd never really had a body till then – until in the last darkness she had had to return to Martin, curled into himself in the shelter they had both made.

How she loved Eduardo! For an afternoon, letting her and the others swim, denying himself that cool water, so that no one would suspect their love. Only Martin knew that when Louise turned to the shore and bent forward, pulling slightly at a bra cup, it was a sign for Eduardo, sitting looking lazily onto the water.

The fish the old man had brought filled the air with a sweet sea smell; the plantain were buried in the ash. The fish was so fresh it crumbled in their hands, white flakes of it that they licked from their open palms. With the plantain, each would be satisfied. As they ate, the sun finally melted into the horizon. Behind them now was the black island; facing them, the silvered light that never quite left the sea.

Eduardo and Rafael finally strode into the water together like father and son. Louise was already there. Her fingers brushed the calm surface of the water, then she span through it, remembering the freedom of that first swim in the forest and him calling her in. Now it was she who had waited for him, calling mockingly, 'What scares you? There are no water snakes here either!'

A ragged cloud began to drift over the surface of the moon, darkening the water.

Eduardo had not reached her when the government forces opened fire. Martin obeyed Jacques' call and hit the sand. He saw El Taino rise and shout – though he could not be sure, it sounded like 'Miguel!' – before two bullets tore out his chest.

From where she stood in the water, Louise saw Rafael, his back to her, charging for the shore. The bullet entered below his armpit and ripped through his ribcage. His blood was a smeared sunset before he fell into the water and Maria screamed his name.

Louise had reached Eduardo, thinking she would envelop him, save him; that together they would surrender. Eduardo knew the government forces better.

'No, Louise, away!'

He was trying to push her from him when there was a burst of gunfire. The first bullet bored a hole through his throat so perfectly that Louise could see framed there a clutch of stars. The second and third bullets sliced through them both. Louise twisted as she fell and pulled Eduardo down on top of her in such a way that it was impossible to tell whether they were fighting each other or embracing.

In the silence that followed, a voice rang out: '*Se acabó! Ríndanse ya!* It's over! Surrender!'

Jacques took Eduardo by his shoulders and hauled him off Louise. All his strength came back to him as he cast Eduardo's body away from her. Jacques cradled her then, his hand stroking her stubbly hair. Melanie laid her head on her daughter's bloody chest and wept.

Maria's arms were raised as she'd been commanded. She clasped her head between her forearms; tears coursed down her cheeks. Below her lay Rafael's long, smooth back: his blood blackened the water around him.

Martin stared out to where Louise was held and where Eduardo floated close by. He felt a secret harden within him. Though his parents embraced him, he stared through the embrace to what he had learned and could not forget. (Much time would have to pass before, as if in the blink of a shutter he had missed, he would be able to see clearly before he'd turned away the look of imperishable relief and gratitude in his mother's eyes.)

Mason, in his crisp fatigues, stepped over Gabriel's body – the staring eyes, the arms outstretched, pleading.

'Jesus, what a fuck-up. You guys don't piss about, do you? Who trained you? The fucking Mafia?'

The leader of the government forces smiled at the compliment. Now they had these new assault rifles, he knew they would have no need of these American 'advisers'.

'Smile all you like,' said Mason, 'but this isn't the kind of wrap-up we wanted.'

'They're enemies, yes, so why cry? You have all the hostages back, I think, alive. Apart from the girl. Pity, nice girl.'

Martin became aware of the distant sounds of car horns voicing their disgruntlement with the snow. He expected school would be cancelled today. Perhaps none of them would have to leave the house. They'd all have breakfast together. Mum, Dad, Nick and he. He'd like that. Then he would sleep. Oh, how he would sleep. He thought back over his night's work. Of course, he too would have to invent dialogue – he had little idea, for example, what Louise and Eduardo had talked about while he lay in the hut, counting lines of stars through the palm fronds in a hopeless attempt to quell his desire. And much else of what he knew had come second-hand. Nor could he swear to the island having sixty types of mango. But for the latter there was the library and for the former, well, invention was the greater part of the novelist's task. For it had dawned on him, sometime in the night, that writing a novel could be the best way to tell his story, while keeping his promise to Louise.

He would have to change the names, of course, but behind the names, he could do something to honour the living and the dead; to arrive at a kind of truth, where Louise could lie in Eduardo's arms again and Rafael know that his words were answered.

'*They will be born and they will die again and be born again. They will never stop being born, because death is a lie.*'

POSTSCRIPT

The woman in the yellow jumpsuit stood in the centre of the small exercise yard, turned her face to the sun and rolled her head five times one way, five times another.

The jumpsuit made her seem larger than she was, for inside its bulk she was slim and sinewy and, for all her privations, still powerful. Though flecks of grey had spread through her black hair, when she brought her head level again, her eyes – fierce, brown – burned through the mesh of wires that surrounded her and fixed on the blue open sea. Out there, they could not catch her, could not hold her. Out there, there were a million whispers, not one of which could they isolate and catch a clear sense of.

Of course they'd tried.

On and off for a year now she'd been held in freezing cages, airless cells, at times manacled and blindfolded, been bombarded by deafening music, denied sleep, threatened with snarling dogs. 'Oh yes, *señora*,' Mason had said, 'I think we'll find somewhere better than *El Castillo* for you – you and all your kind.' She'd lost count of the number of times she'd been interrogated by government officials or Americans with bad Spanish about her links with political subversives or terrorists. She had endured it all and been brought again, once each episode was over, into this small yard, alone, to gaze on the perfect sea.

And even at those times when she had been denied this, her one true communion, she had found she could sit in her cell, on her mattress, and conjure up the sea around her. The walls faded, everything faded, till she was alone – but never lonely.

For if it were anywhere, that's where his spirit was: it was the sea into which his blood had poured and the bloodied sea that washed his island now – as it had long before the first Taino people, arriving in their simple canoes, had named it *Caguama*, the great sea turtle. The sea would not let the island forget Rafael. Of its million whispers Caguama must by now have heard every one.

Today, though, when the sea smiles, Maria smiles

back, for she will soon be close to it without this wire mesh between them. A guard, realizing there is a prospect of change in the air, has brought her up to date on a rapidly developing situation.

It seems the anti-terrorist concerns, which had seen universal approval for the American-backed action against the Portuondo hostage-takers, have been challenged in the liberal west. Slowly a number of independent journalists have ascertained the viciousness of the action; discovered not a military engagement but a 'MASSACRE'.

For that is the word that has been taken up by the press in general. It was a way to make the story run. Then the publication of the diaries of one of the hostages had led to a rash of linked articles and profiles. 'MASSACRE' was at times in these substituted by 'BLOOD-BATH'. In short, a local horror had become international.

Attention had then focused not only on the US role, but on United Nickel, the American company which had, in the words of one article, 'plundered the land and impoverished its people'. One investigative journalist had traced the mother of a local man who had colluded with both the guerrillas and the authorities. Her husband had been a worker at United Nickel. Now her husband and her son were dead. What had this poor, innocent woman – Pilar Ferrer – done to deserve such tragedies in her life?

General Quitano felt he had to act against 'this predatory company that thinks it can ride roughshod over our people'. He would not wait for the promised commission. There followed a number of incendiary speeches, stressing his independence of judgement, his country's rights and their long history of independence from foreign intervention. You could see how puffed up these speeches made him feel; in the same way as you could see emotion ravage him when he mentioned the disloyalty of those within his own family.

'My own nephew,' his voice cracked, 'whom I taught to pitch and to swing a bat . . . that he should betray me . . .'

A puffed-up little runt – well, Mason had always known that. But his unreliability was a more serious affair.

The orders went out to withdraw US support – military and economic – from General Quitano's government. Who did they think they were, turning on an American company like that? It was a point of principle, though not one that troubled Mason a great deal. Because it wasn't the endgame yet. It rarely was the endgame in his experience. Already opposition to the Quitano regime was beginning to gather around the guerrilla leader's exiled mother, Mercedes Portuondo (Quitano). The networks broadcast interviews with her in which she came across as articulate and dignified.

'The lives Pilar Ferrer and I have lived have been very different. But in two respects we are alike. Each of us has lost a loved husband and a son . . . and each of us yearns for peace on our island, true independence from foreign interference and the liberty of those who have opposed the present regime.'

Mason sniffed. *Paz! Independencia! Libertad! That* old threesome again. Still, there was a chance, if things worked out, that Señora Portuondo would be more congenial to deal with; more reliable than her opportunistic brother-in-law had proved to be. Some day a US Air Force aeroplane would be waiting to take her back to Santa Clara. In the meantime Mason's bag was already packed – sneakers, snorkel, camera – for another field in Central America.

* * *

Maria finished her exercise routine with twenty-five trunk curls. Beads of sweat trickled from her armpits down the sides of her ribcage. But her breath was even. Calm. She felt her jumpsuit loose about her, like a skin to be sloughed off.

'It won't be long now,' she whispered to the sea. 'All the bad apples will fall. Soon, *mi compañero . . . mi amor*.'

The bones of the dead ask
As if in prayer
What have you done
With our gifts? The wind
Thickens in the south. Clear your throat –
It is time you prepared an answer.

ABOUT THE AUTHOR

Tom Pow is the award-winning author of four books of poetry (*Rough Seas, The Moth Trap, Red Letter Day* and *Landscapes and Legacies*). He has also written three radio plays, a travel book about Peru (*In the Palace of Serpents*), and three picture books (*Who Is the World For?, Callum's Big Day* and *Tell Me One Thing, Dad*). In 2003 *Scabbit Isle*, his first novel for young adults, was published, followed by *The Pack* in 2004.

Tom Pow was the Writer in Residence at the Edinburgh International Book Festival from 2001 to 2003. He works at Glasgow University Crichton Campus in Dumfries, where he teaches courses in creative writing and storytelling.

Abandoned by a cold world, they must trust one another – or die . . .

Bradley, Victor and Floris live with the dogs on the dark, forgotten edge of a segregated city. Haunted by memories and abandoned by society, they have learned to survive on their own. But when Floris is kidnapped the others must venture into the unknown to save their friend. It is a journey fraught with danger – violent gangs stalk the streets, and corrupt warlords viciously guard their territories. But it is also a journey of discovery . . .

0 099 47563 4
978 0 099 47563 7

How far would you go to save another's soul?

'It almost appeared as if she were waiting for me. Whether it was some movement of her head, a hand slightly raised that signalled her expectancy, I can't remember now, though it was enough to convince me there was something more here than a case of mistaken identity.'

The first time Sam sees the mysterious girl, she vanishes into the deserted fields beyond the town. Centuries before, this was the place to which plague victims were banished, a place of unspeakable terror – Scabbit Isle. Gradually Sam uncovers the horror of the girl's story, which seems somehow linked to his own.

0 552 54986 X
978 0 552 54986 8